The Secret of Grim Hill

Published by Lobster Press™
1620 Sherbrooke Street West, Suites C & D
Montréal, Québec   H3H 1C9
Tel. (514) 904-1100 • Fax (514) 904-1101 • www.lobsterpress.com

Publisher: Alison Fripp
Editors: Alison Fripp & Meghan Nolan
Editorial Assistants: Katie Scott & Olga Zoumboulis
Cover Illustration: John Shroades
Graphic Design & Production: Tammy Desnoyers

We acknowledge the financial support of the Government of Canada
through the Book Publishing Industry Development Program (BPIDP)
for our publishing activities.

We acknowledge the support of the Canada
Council for the Arts for our publishing program.

The Canada Council   Le Conseil des Arts
for the Arts   du Canada

Library and Archives Canada Cataloguing in Publication

DeMeulemeester, Linda, date
        The secret of Grim Hill / Linda DeMeulemeester.

ISBN-13: 978-1-897073-53-7
ISBN-10: 1-897073-53-4

        I. Title.

PS8607.E58S43 2007   jC813'.6   C2006-905109-7

Ghostbusters is a trademark of Columbia Pictures Industries; **Guinness Book of
World Records** is a trademark of Arthur Guinness and Sons; **MSN** is a trademark
of Microsoft Corporation; **Slinky** is a trademark of James Industries, Inc.

To my sweethearts John, Alec, and Joey

Acknowledgements: Huge gratitude to my friend Janine Cross for her sharp eye for action and adventure. Much appreciation to Eileen Kernaghan and Helix for their encouragement and support. Many thanks to Meghan Nolan for her great editorial feedback.

– Linda DeMeulemeester

The Secret of Grim Hill

written by
Linda DeMeulemeester

Lobster Press ™

CHAPTER 1

The Wish

PEOPLE ALWAYS SAY, "Be careful what you wish for." But from that first moment, I didn't care. I wished I could be anywhere but in my new school, Darkmont High.

It was as if I was in one of those weird dreams. You know the ones where you're in school standing in front of your locker, but you're in your underwear. You can't remember your lock combination. The bell has rung and you're late for class.

Except for the underwear thing, it wasn't a dream. After spinning the combination for about the twentieth time, my lock finally clicked, but the hallway had already cleared. When I wrenched my locker open, it clanged against the wall. Okay, the hall wasn't completely empty. A teacher shook his head at me as he walked past. I blushed, opened my binder, and checked my new schedule. Naturally my first class was up two floors.

"Crap," I muttered and took off in a hurry.

The gloomy stairwell was so dark I could hardly see, but that didn't stop me from leaping up the stairs two at a time.

"Hold it right there. No running in the

building!" shouted another teacher. When I turned around and saw the dark blue suit and steel-gray hair, I recognized the vice principal, Ms. Sevren, who had registered me the day before. She caught up with me and said, "You must walk in an orderly fashion the rest of the way," and followed me to make sure that was exactly what I did.

Five more minutes passed before I knocked on the classroom door. Nothing happened, so I swallowed the lump in my throat and knocked even louder. The door opened and a dark-haired girl impatiently waved me in.

"New student?" asked the teacher, who was wearing a lab coat.

I nodded.

"Name?" She didn't even look up from the board.

"Cat Peters," I said.

Everyone stared at me. The teacher turned around.

"Cat?" she asked. A few people giggled.

"It's short for Caitlin." Nobody in my old school thought my name was funny. Why did we have to move to this stupid town?

"Well ... um ... *Cat*, I'm Ms. Dreeble. Find a seat quickly." She grabbed the registration form from my hand.

I looked for a place to sit, but none of the lab tables had an empty seat.

"Sit down. You're disrupting the class." Ms. Dreeble tapped the board with her chalk. Tap ... tap ... Everyone waited. Sweat collected under my armpits, and I pulled at my beige sweater. A lone stool was in the far corner near a bookcase stacked with Bunsen burners.

The class was so cluttered that I tripped over several book bags as I made my way to the stool. The students giggled again. Miserably, I huddled on my seat and tucked my backpack underneath.

"Who is your homeroom teacher?" Ms. Dreeble said and frowned.

When I didn't answer, she asked me again.

I'd registered at this new school yesterday, one week past the start of the fall term. I'd had to wait for all my school records to get transferred. Then I missed homeroom this morning because I couldn't open my locker. I had no idea who my homeroom teacher was.

"I'm not sure," I muttered.

"Well aren't *you* the bright one?" the teacher said and rolled her eyes.

Laughter rattled around the class. My stomach ached and sweat dribbled down my back – my stupid sweater was so hot.

Ms. Dreeble finished writing a list of lab instructions on the board and said, "Class, before you begin today's science lab, I want you to review these safety rules with your partners."

The class filled with chatter, and I could smell the faint odor of gas as students turned Bunsen burners on and off. When I walked by other tables in an attempt to find a partner, everyone turned away. Ms. Dreeble didn't seem to notice or care, so I sat back down on my stool and stared at the only poster in the whole room: a wrinkled, dog-eared chart of the periodic table. I got as far as uranium's atomic weight when the bell rang.

As I rushed past her, Ms. Dreeble called me back to her desk. The other kids filed out of the classroom.

"You didn't hand in today's lab. You've lost ten marks on your first day." Ms. Dreeble's eyes kept blinking behind her thick glasses. "A poor start, don't you think ... *Cat*?"

"Tell me about it," I said under my breath as I walked out the door. I checked my schedule and noticed that Mr. Morrows's history class was on the same floor, which meant I could get there quickly and find a spot right away. History would go better. It had to.

This time, there were lots of seats to choose from because I'd arrived first. Not too far back and definitely not too close to the front, I selected a desk positioned perfectly in the middle. After I sat down, lots of students poured into the classroom. This place was much more crowded than my old school. I stretched my legs out from under the cramped desk.

"Blue jeans are not allowed," Mr. Morrows said as he pointed to me. "Only colored denim."

For the first time, I noticed that none of the other kids wore blue jeans. They wore brown or black ones, or khakis, and some girls even wore skirts. What else could I do wrong?

"Sorry," I sighed. Money was tight with the move, and I wondered if Mom had enough money left in the budget for new pants. I began to sweat again and pulled off my sweater.

"No, no, this won't do. You can't wear that either. Come up here." Mr. Morrows folded his arms and glared at me, his gray mustache twitching.

"Now what?" I whispered – okay, I said it out loud. I stood up and pulled down my T-shirt, which had gotten a bit too small over the summer.

"Your midriff is showing," the teacher said in shock.

I quickly checked my front and relaxed a bit. He just meant that some of my stomach showed.

"Take my advice – go home for lunch and change your clothes," said Mr. Morrows. "Otherwise, a hall monitor will give you detention. Students must obey the dress code – no blue jeans, no short tops." His mouth made an annoying smacking noise as he *tsk-tsked*.

I stared at him in disbelief, wondering how

he could be so unfair. As soon as the lunch bell rang, I threw my pen and binder into my backpack and rushed out of class ahead of everyone. When I slammed the door, it bounced back open behind me.

"That attitude will get you a suspension, miss!" Mr. Morrows called after me. I didn't look back.

In my other town, in my old school, I never once got in trouble. It seemed as if the teachers here wouldn't even give me a chance.

When I finally reached my locker, it only took three tries this time to open it. I grabbed my lunch and headed to the cafeteria. It appeared that no one else went to their locker first because by the time I got to the lunchroom, it was packed.

As I circled the tables, none of the students that I'd seen in my earlier classes acknowledged me or opened up a space for me. My stomach knotted. At the far end of the room, a red-haired girl from my history class sat alone at a small table. She was studying a strange looking flyer that had a creepy sketch of a witch on it. When she didn't glance up at me, I kept walking.

Suddenly I heard, "Hey, Cat, come sit over here!"

I spotted Jasper Chung doing his homework. Jasper had skipped a grade, which made him twelve, a year younger than me. He wore his hair spiked in last year's style and sported not-too-trendy black-rimmed glasses. Because he lived next door, he was the only one I'd met in town so far. Still, I hung out with the cool group at my old school – I wasn't quite ready to sit with a younger boy. Instead, I waved goodbye, deciding to take Mr. Morrows's advice and go home to change. As I walked through the door, I noticed another girl holding the same odd witch flyer.

Outside in the tiny gray box of a courtyard, I kept thinking about how before we moved, my life had been so much better. "I want to be popular again!" I shouted. A few crows on a tree branch above my head flew away. No one else noticed my complaint.

I couldn't help but think that it might be different if I could attend the private school where my mom worked. Grimoire School was closer to my house and sat atop the wooded hill, which everyone called Grim Hill, partly because of the name of the school, and partly because it was a dark and creepy place. But the school itself was a beautiful stone building that had been around forever, and it was pretty fancy. Since Grimoire was an all-girls private school, everyone wore a uniform – no one had to worry about wearing the right clothes. Plus, it was expensive to go there, so they could probably afford nicer teachers.

That school sounded exciting and fun. My

mom had mentioned that the classrooms were often empty because the students took field trips all the time. What's more, I loved sports, and the school had amazing athletic facilities. To top it all off, the kids who went there weren't from this town, so a new person could fit in and not have to worry that she hasn't known everyone since kindergarten.

If only I could go *there* ... I shook my head. There were only two high schools in town, and that one, Grimoire, cost a fortune. "I *wish* I could go to Grimoire!" I told the crows. But I knew there was no hope.

One of the crows fluttered by and landed on top of a signpost. Then another crow landed on the sign, and another. Below the three crows was a poster with the same eerie, green-faced witch that I'd seen on those flyers in the cafeteria. When I walked over for a closer look, the witch had a sly smile and seemed to be grinning right at me. The poster advertised a Halloween soccer match.

"This can't be true." Because I wasn't exactly having a run of luck since my parents divorced, I tried not to get excited. But my heart beat faster anyway.

Grimoire School was sponsoring the soccer match. Tryouts were next week after school. Athletic scholarships to Grimoire would be awarded to everyone on the winning team. If I made the team and won, I could be attending Grimoire by December!

I'd never heard about anyone winning a scholarship from a single soccer game, but so what? This was my chance! I'd do anything to get away from Darkmont High – anything.

Before I raced home, I hesitated for a second and looked back at the poster.

I swear the crows on top of the sign were laughing at me.

CHAPTER 2

Dark Days at Darkmont

AS I WALKED home to change my clothes, I couldn't stop thinking about the Grimoire scholarship. What if I didn't make the team? In the meantime, just in case, I decided to put more effort into fitting in at Darkmont. That meant going back to school and actually trying to make friends, not to mention making an effort to get along better with my teachers. A positive attitude, that's all I needed. By the time I climbed up the steps to my front porch, I was feeling better.

Our new house wasn't really new. It was old and drafty with plank wood flooring and big rooms with high ceilings. We used to live in a modern condo with elevators and a big activity room. This place was okay, though. For one thing, my little sister, Sookie, and I didn't have to worry about being too loud and bothering the neighbors below.

Up in my room, I grabbed a top that fit a lot less snug and wouldn't ride up. I wasn't so lucky with pants. I couldn't find anything in my closet but jeans. There were still a lot of unpacked boxes in Sookie's closet, so I went to take a look.

Sookie's room was across the hall from mine.

Her sheets and blankets lay tangled in a knot in the middle of the floor. I heard her hamster, Buddy, skittering on his wheel and noticed that Sookie's room didn't look much better than the inside of Buddy's cage. I checked his water bottle and brushed the cedar chips out of his seed dish. At least she always made sure her hamster had food and water. Suddenly, the bird in Sookie's cuckoo clock let me know that it was already past lunch hour. Walking home from Darkmont had taken a lot longer than I'd realized.

I rushed out of Sookie's room, slid down the wide oak banister, hurried out of the house, and ran down the tree-lined street, crunching through the fallen gold- and crimson-colored leaves. Stopping for a second, I glanced up past the woods to the top of Grim Hill.

Grimoire School looked like a castle against the pale blue sky. It would be so much faster to climb that hill every day than walk more than a mile across town to Darkmont High. I wouldn't have to wake up until the last minute, which would be great because I'm not exactly a morning person.

I shook my head. What I had to do was focus on making life at Darkmont better ... somehow. I hurried back to school.

When I finally got there, my teacher sent me to the office because I was really late after lunch. But this time, I didn't slam any doors or stomp off.

Instead, I apologized and went promptly to the vice principal.

"That's one demerit for tardiness," said Ms. Sevren. "And while we're at it, one demerit for wearing pants that don't fit the dress code – you've had time to realize we have a 'no blue jeans' policy."

This seemed completely unfair, but I didn't let myself get angry. Instead, I smiled and said sorry.

"Remember, um ... Caitlin," Ms. Sevren began.

This made me flinch because someone calling me "Caitlin" instead of "Cat" always means something serious.

"Five demerit points equals a full week of detention," warned Ms. Sevren. She stared over her glasses at me until I gulped and returned to class.

By the time the last bell of the day sounded, no one in the entire school had said a single word to me. It was as if I was invisible when I stood by my locker. I slung my bag over my shoulder and walked home.

* * *

The next morning, I was determined my day would go better. For starters, the night before, Mom had helped me dig through a bunch of boxes, and I found a pair of white capris. I wore a black T-shirt that sat below my belly button – the outfit totally complied with the dress code. I arrived early and went straight to the student recreation room to check which teams or clubs I could join.

"Sorry, we don't have a soccer, basketball, or volleyball team," said the adviser.

"What about field hockey ... or a swim team?" I asked.

She shook her head. "Sorry."

"Is there a school choir or band?" I asked.

"Not enough students signed up, so those activities were canceled." She smiled apologetically. "We're looking for lunch monitors and library helpers."

"I'll think about it," I said unconvincingly. Okay, so I couldn't meet other students by joining any activities. Maybe if I acted super friendly, people would talk to me.

When I walked down the hall, I smiled at everyone. Perhaps I was overdoing it a bit, because I got some strange looks.

In science, I tried hard to have a positive attitude, but things were only getting worse. Still no one volunteered to be my lab partner, so once again I was stuck on the stool at the back of the class. And then Ms. Dreeble announced, "Sorry class, but the photocopier and projector are broken. You'll have to copy all the notes off the board." She began to scribble, and chalk dust filled the air. She covered blackboard after blackboard with tiny notes. I had to keep getting up from my seat to read the board.

"For goodness' sakes, Cat," said Ms. Dreeble. "Stop hopping up and down. You're disrupting the class. Find a seat closer to the board if you need to see better."

There weren't any seats closer to the board, so I had no choice but to stay on the same stool and finish copying all the notes until my eyes ached from the strain and my hand cramped from all the writing. "Positive attitude," I kept chanting to myself right up until the class was over.

During history, Mr. Morrows announced, "Our field trips have been canceled, and there's no money to upgrade our video machine to a DVD player. That's what I'd planned for all the movies, so we'll have to stick to extra readings."

Everyone sighed and opened their workbooks.

"Where's your workbook, Cat?" He came up beside me and checked over my shoulder.

No one had said anything about a workbook. Shuffling through my pile of books, I discovered a sheet of paper that listed all the extra materials I was supposed to have bought for this term.

"You're going to lose even more marks today," Mr. Morrows said as he walked away.

It was getting more difficult to stay positive, but I didn't crack. This time, I didn't mutter or sigh, and at lunch I kept my cheerful smile. But I made sure I didn't smile at every single person, only every other person.

It worked! At one table, maybe the cutest guy at Darkmont – I think his name was Zach – waved for me to join his group. My heart beat in relief. This was more like my old life.

Saying hi to everyone, I walked toward the table. But the second I started to slide into the empty seat, a girl came out of nowhere and sat down. She'd been right behind me. Zach had been waving at her – not me.

Everyone at the table giggled as I crouched beside her with my tray in my hand. I turned quickly to leave, lost my footing, and watched in horror as my tray tipped and a plate and glass smashed to the floor, shattering. Of course, ketchup and grape juice spattered all down my white pants. Everyone in the lunchroom began pounding the tables and laughing while I backed away. Out of the corner of my eye, I spotted my neighbor, Jasper, who wasn't laughing. Instead, he winced in sympathy, but his pity didn't help.

When I ran outside into the courtyard, a wind was blowing drifts of crunchy dry leaves into little tornadoes. A half-torn poster fluttered by and stuck to the ketchup on my capris. *Just great.* I pulled the flyer off and turned it over. The witch's face now dripped in ketchup blood. Her wicked smile stared up at me – it seemed as if she had joined the cackles that rattled around the room behind me. That didn't matter. What mattered was that underneath her creepy face was the notice for Grimoire School soccer tryouts.

Nothing was going to stop me from making the team, winning the scholarship to Grimoire, and getting out of this stupid school! Nothing.

* * *

That night at dinner, after replaying my day in gruesome detail, my little sister asked, "You mean, the teachers here think you're a troublemaker?"

"I think so," I said feeling miserable.

"Every kid laughed at you when you slipped?" asked Sookie.

I nodded. "And I had to go home and change yet again. And even though I ran both ways to make it back in time, I got one more demerit for wearing jeans." My voice broke.

Sookie brushed a blond strand of hair from her face and slammed her fork onto her plate. "That's despicable!"

Sookie had an interesting vocabulary for an eight-year-old.

Mom said, "Cat, I'm sorry you had another rough day. I can see you're even more determined to try out for the soccer match now, but remember, it's more than that. You would also have to win the game to get the scholarship." Then Mom got an odd look on her face. "Grimoire has unbelievable facilities and amazing resources. I can't begin to list them, but ..." She hesitated and didn't finish what she was going to say. Instead she said, "You know what I always tell you two."

"Don't put all your eggs in one basket," Sookie chimed.

"Cat?" Mom waited.

I nodded, but I didn't mean it. I'd given Darkmont a chance. Grimoire *had* to be a hundred times better. The soccer match was the only thing that mattered. I was going to put all of my eggs in the Grimoire basket.

Later that night, Mom helped me bleach my white pants and promised she'd buy me a few more pairs soon. My alarm was set extra early to give me plenty of time to get to school, and my binder was stuffed with every possible worksheet. In order to make it to the tryouts on Monday, I had to stay detention free for the rest of the week.

* * *

All went well until Friday morning when Mom was called into work early.

"You'll have to take Sookie to school," Mom said. She grabbed her purse, kissed us goodbye, and hurried out the door before I could say a word.

My little sister crunched her frosty oats, one oat at a time.

"Gulp that down," I told her. "My school begins fifteen minutes earlier than yours."

She didn't eat any faster.

"C'mon Sookie, we have to go!" I checked the clock.

"I have to find my hamster ball. I need it for show-and-tell." Sookie left the table and spent ten minutes rummaging in her room.

"Hurry!" I shouted.

"I can't find it!" she called down.

I leaped up the stairs – two at a time – to help her. We found the hamster ball under her bed. She grabbed it, and we hurried out of the house and down the street.

After I dropped Sookie off at school, I raced all the way to Darkmont. If I cut through the custodian's door at the back, I'd make it to my locker before the second bell. We weren't supposed to go in that way, but I checked to make sure no one was watching.

When I came up out of the basement, I bumped straight into Ms. Sevren.

"That door's an out-of-bounds area, Caitlin. That means you get *two* demerits instead of one. That's *five* demerit points now."

My heart banged against my chest.

"You've got a week's detention, beginning

today," said Ms. Sevren.

Detention? How was I going to make it to the Grimoire soccer tryouts now?

CHAPTER 3

Dying to Make the Team

THAT WEEKEND WHEN I slept, I dreamed of glory. I'd kick, and soccer balls would fly off my feet and go straight into the goals. Crowds would cheer. Girls on my team would pound me on the back and high-five me. Then I'd wake up and the cold, cruel reality – that I had detention on Monday, the day of the Grimoire soccer tryouts – would settle in.

When Monday morning came, I squirmed in my desk seat. I couldn't concentrate as I thought of a million excuses to skip detention – that I had a sore throat, or I had to pick up my sister from school, or I had a dentist appointment. The problem was that there was no guarantee anyone would believe me.

Then it occurred to me. Maybe it was easier to beg for forgiveness after skipping detention than to ask for permission to back out.

At the end of last period, before the principal announced my name for detention over the loudspeaker, I asked the teacher if I could get a drink of water. When I left the classroom, I kept walking down the long hall and out onto the street without looking back. In all my school years, I'd never disobeyed a teacher, let alone a vice principal. But I was happy to pay the price, which of course was going to be high because there was also the small matter of skipping the last fifteen minutes of school as well as a detention. Now I understood what people meant by a "slippery slope."

"Is school already over?" asked Mr. Keating, the grocer, who was standing outside his store.

I started running.

"Hey!" he said gruffly. "What are you up to?"

Blood was still rushing through my ears after I'd arrived home. I went to Sookie's room and started tossing boxes out of her closet, looking for my soccer cleats. It took awhile, but I finally found them.

When I heard Mom and Sookie come in downstairs, I looked up at the clock. I had to rush if I wanted to be on time for the tryouts.

"What'cha doing?" asked Sookie as she ran up the stairs. She didn't even mention the horrible mess I'd made on her bedroom floor.

"I'm heading to soccer tryouts." I had to hurry.

"Mom's going for groceries. She wants you to watch me." Sookie's dimpled face turned into a worried frown.

"How about you watch me at the tryouts?" I managed a half-smile, worrying that Mr. Keating would tell my mother I'd run off early from school.

Sookie nodded excitedly and tucked her short hair behind her ears. "How old do you have to be to play?"

"More than eight," I said.

Sookie frowned again. "I'm never old enough for anything fun."

Sookie and I left the house and hiked up Grim Hill to the soccer field. A pale mist flowed through the tree leaves, which were turning a kaleidoscope of rusts, reds, oranges, and yellows. Like cotton candy, the wisps of gray mist floated down the hill and collected in patches.

Once we got to the top of the hill, the air was perfectly clear. Red-berried bushes poked through patches of dark fir trees. Golden sunlit paths circled around the school.

"Wouldn't you *love* to go to this school?" I asked as I tugged Sookie along. Sookie slowed down.

"I don't think so," said Sookie. "No, not one bit." Sookie had stopped in front of a little shelter between the school and the soccer field. It looked as if it had been a picnic area once. But now the table and benches were covered with thorns and weeds.

"I'd especially stay away from this spot. It feels all wrong," Sookie whispered. Her blue eyes widened. She turned and looked into the tall stained-glass windows of the school. It was as if she could almost see something there, something she didn't like very much.

"Hurry up!" I pulled her away, not thinking about her strange comment. The tryouts had already begun and the field below swarmed with about fifty girls chasing after soccer balls.

"C'mon, Sookie!" I collapsed on a bench and started to lace up my soccer boots. "Ouch!"

"What's wrong?" asked Sookie. She walked over and sat down on the bench beside me.

"My boots," I said as I bent over to loosen the laces. "My feet must have grown a couple of sizes since last season. These things are squeezing my toes."

"Just wear your shoes," suggested Sookie.

"They're too smooth on the bottom. I'll slip without cleats." I said this kind of sharply out of frustration, but it wasn't Sookie's fault; she was just trying to help. I felt a pinch of guilt, but not as big a pinch as when I walked in my dumb cleats. I loosened the laces some more, then left Sookie behind on the bench. I raced out onto the field where I was just one more girl chasing after the ball.

I had made it onto the best soccer team at my old school last year, but I was starting to realize that whatever I'd accomplished in my last town didn't count for much now. As if to prove this, my foot cramped, my legs tangled under me, and I went flying. I sat up and brushed the moist grass from my shirt, wanting to explain to anyone who would listen that this wasn't really me, that I was a good soccer player. They'd want me on the team if they only knew!

The coach, a thin woman with long, black hair and chalk-white skin came up to me. "Do you think sitting on the field is the way to play the game?" She checked off something on her chart.

I got a sinking feeling.

The coach then raised a whistle from around her neck and blew a shrill blast. "Girls, form a line. I want to see your kick shots."

I hesitated, and she looked down at me.

"You do know how to kick the ball, don't you?" The coach shook her head and went over to stand with the rest of the girls who were quickly lining up.

I stood, shook my arms and legs, and imagined getting rid of the bad energy. I'd heard that somewhere: *Think happy thoughts*. Well, no happy thoughts rushed into my brain, but I was moving again, and I joined the lineup of other hopeful players. I noticed the two girls I'd seen in the lunchroom studying the witch-face flyers. Guess I wasn't the only one who wanted out of Darkmont.

Every girl began to take shots on the goal, but when they kicked, no one got any balls into the net. When it was my turn, I squared off in front of the Grimoire goalie. She wore shorts and a jersey that had the school colors of black with orange and purple pinstripes, and although she wasn't that big, she leaped so high and fast, she almost flew.

I swallowed the butterflies that tried to jump out of my stomach, and I gave one of my old soccer tricks a shot. I stared at the girl guarding the goal. First I imagined she was one of those kids who'd laughed at me in the lunchroom. But that just got me mad so I saw her for what she was, the person trying to keep me out of the school of my dreams. Then the strangest feeling came over me.

Time felt frozen, as if the world had stopped spinning, and excitement bubbled up inside me. I just knew something good was going to happen. All my senses felt as if they were hooked up to an amplifier, and I was blasted by the autumn day. Colored leaves blazed from the branches. Woodsmoke and the damp smell of wet leaves tickled my nose. A winged rush from a murder of crows flew over my head, and when I licked my lips, I tasted pumpkin pie. The sensations were so overpowering, they blocked out my throbbing toes.

The goalie could instantly dodge high and wide, so instead, I picked an area closer to the ground and hoped it was a weak spot. My foot launched the ball. Okay, on T.V. the kicks are perfect and the soccer ball drops behind the goalie every time. This was real life. But it didn't matter. My goal was perfect. A bunch of girls even clapped!

The two coaches walked toward me, scribbling

furiously on their clipboards. They looked like identical twins, except one had straight white hair instead of black. They introduced themselves as Ms. Maliss and Ms. Sinster, and then they both shook my hand. Even though they had an icy grip, I felt warm all over.

For the rest of the practice, I ran fast, kicked hard, and scored goals. Before the practice finished, the two coaches posted a list on the fence by the dugout and blew their whistles.

"Here are the two teams for the big soccer game," announced Ms. Sinster, the one with the long black hair. "The Witches and the Ghosts," she said as she pointed to the rosters. "The names circled in red have made the teams."

We swarmed up to the lists, pushing and shoving – I guess *many* of us wanted to win the scholarship to Grimoire School. Eventually I made my way to the front and skimmed the list until I spotted "Cat Peters!" My name was circled in bloodred ink and "Witches" had been written beside it. Hope thrilled up from my aching feet and looped through each strand of my brown hair. I'd made it. I couldn't wait to go home and tell ... *oops*. I remembered what I was supposed to be doing instead of playing soccer. *Sookie!*

In the last hour, I hadn't checked on my sister once, even though I was responsible for her. When I went over to the bench where I'd left her, she wasn't there. My heart beat wildly as I raced around scanning the field – no Sookie!

I ran to the other end of the field where I spotted her sitting in the bleachers. Relief poured through me. How could I have been so stupid to forget about my little sister?

Sookie was sitting beside a girl who was about my age. She looked like a Goth girl with her jet-black bangs and straight hair, pale blue eyes, and odd, old-fashioned black clothes – really odd clothes: a skirt down past her knees, long stockings pulled up high, pointy ankle boots, and a long striped sweater that was belted low on her hips. The girl stared at me. Not just at me, but right through me. It was as if I would have felt her watching me even if I had my back turned to her. It was nerve-racking.

"I made the team, short stuff! I played great after all." I hugged Sookie partly in excitement, but mostly in relief that she hadn't wandered off.

"Cindy says she knew the school would pick you," Sookie said almost in a whisper. "She says that's why you'd better be careful."

"What?" I turned to the weird girl, who hadn't said a word but kept right on watching me with those freaky eyes. When she finally turned her head, I noticed she had a strange silver hair clip that was like a spider web, and it had a tiny little ruby spider in the middle. Suddenly, the coaches blew their whistles again. They hauled two huge boxes out onto the field and started handing out the most dazzling uniforms I had ever seen. I grabbed Sookie's hand and we ran up to get a closer look.

The Ghosts' uniforms shimmered silvery white – they were wicked! The Witches' uniforms were even better. The shorts had a front flap over them. Mom called this type of thing a skort. The skirt part had a ragged hem and was a black, silky material. The long, black, witch-fire green striped socks would come up just past my knees. The jersey matched the socks, black with green stripes.

I bundled my uniform under my arm. The mist started rolling faster down the hill, which meant we had to go before it became too foggy.

"Sookie, I am about to become a 'Witch!'"

"This isn't such a good idea," said Sookie. "Cindy says you'd better watch out – that the school has secrets."

"What?" I was too excited to wonder what Sookie meant, but I looked for the Goth girl on the bleachers.

She had disappeared into the mist.

Chapter 4

A Fog Descends

THAT NIGHT, A thick fog settled around the town, but by morning it disappeared. I walked to school under a butterscotch sun and the kind of clear sky that comes with a crisp snap in the air. Despite the beautiful morning, I lagged behind the other students streaming into the schoolyard, mostly on account of the rock sitting in my stomach.

I was doomed after skipping class and detention. Sure, thinking about having made the Witches took an edge off my dread, but I knew I was going to be in big trouble.

Once I stepped inside Darkmont High, a group of girls waited for me in front of my locker. Was this some kind of gang meant to drag me to detention hall?

"Are you Cat? You made the team, right?" said the red-haired girl I'd seen at the soccer tryouts.

I nodded cautiously on both counts.

"I'm Mia. I'm on your team." She smiled.

"Me, too," the other girl said as she held out her hand. "I'm Amarjeet. Nice to meet you."

The girls began talking all at once.

"You made the team? I didn't," said one

35

girl sadly.

"Lots of girls didn't make it," said another. Then she turned to me and said, "You must be an awesome soccer player."

"She is an awesome player," said Mia. "She has a wicked shot."

"Wouldn't it be cool to win the scholarship?" said Amarjeet.

"Want to meet us at lunch in the cafeteria?" several of the girls asked simultaneously.

My head spun around as I smiled, answered, and nodded, enjoying all the attention – that is, until the bell rang and everyone scattered. *Great.* I hadn't even gotten around to fiddling with my lock. Now I was going to be late for science – again. But my locker opened instantly, and I grabbed my books and ran. Then I pulled to a dead stop.

Ms. Sevren stood at the foot of the stairs. My heart fluttered as if a bunch of butterflies had gone wild in my chest. *So what? I made the team*, I said to myself – that was worth the 150 demerits she would probably give me. Were vice principals allowed to give detention straight through the entire year?

"Is it true you made the Grimoire team, Cat?" Ms. Sevren asked, peering over her glasses at me.

Convinced she was planning a particularly horrible torture, I nodded and gulped.

"Congratulations," she said and smiled before

walking away.

For a minute, I couldn't move – I was shocked. That is, until the second bell rang. Then I knew I'd better hurry, but not wanting to push my luck, I climbed the stairs in an orderly fashion.

When I stepped into the crowded science classroom, chairs scraped against the floor as people made room for me at their tables. Everyone began talking to me at once.

"Sit with me, Cat."

"We made room for you here."

"Hey, you can join us."

It was kind of funny; now everyone wanted me as a lab partner, but I still didn't know where to sit.

After my lab, I walked to history with Mia. When we opened our textbooks, Mr. Morrows pointed at me. I steeled myself. Even though I had gotten around to buying the proper workbook, we were still not exactly on good terms – he was sure to blow up. Instead he asked, "Cat, would you begin the discussion on what technological advances the Egyptians made for civilization?"

I wasn't exactly prepared for that.

"Um …" I racked my brain. "The Egyptians constructed … um …"

"That's right, Cat. The Egyptians were responsible for construction and irrigation. Excellent." Mr. Morrows beamed at me.

Okay, that was confusing, but I nodded knowingly anyway and stared down at my desk, blushing in relief.

In English class, Ms. Cadly asked, "What does 'bucolic' mean?"

When she pointed to me, I almost fainted. Last week she'd completely ignored me.

"Um … really sick, like when people got the plague?" I finished weakly, not having the slightest idea what "bucolic" meant.

"Excellent. Class, note how Cat used deductive reasoning to figure out the origins of the word. She combined bubonic and colic – plague and illness."

"So that's what the word means?" I said, surprised but rather proud of myself.

"Oh, not at all," said Ms. Cadly. "It means a beautiful landscape of trees and fields. But great deductive skills, Cat."

The class nodded as if they were impressed, which was strange considering I had given the completely wrong answer. But I wasn't about to question my new luck. When the bell rang, I practically floated out of the classroom on a cloud of glory.

At lunch, everyone made room for me at their tables. Teachers walked by saying, "Congratulations, I heard you made the team."

Nobody seemed to remember that I'd skipped

detention the day before.

Zach, who *was* the cutest guy at Darkmont, the one who'd laughed at me last week, said, "I hear you have a wicked shot."

My heart was pounding way too hard for me to do anything but grin. This was more like my old school again back home, except much better.

Emily, a girl from the Ghosts, came up and offered me her hand. "May the best team win," she said, glancing around the crowded, dingy cafeteria, and wrinkling her nose at the heavy odors of grease and cabbage.

"Okay, I don't really mean that," Emily said laughing. "The Ghosts *have* to win, though who can blame anyone for wanting a ticket out of here." Still, her laugh was friendly as she shook my hand. Emily, with the required blond hair and designer clothes, was the most popular girl in eighth grade. And she was being nice to me. Last week she'd made that wrinkled nose when I passed her in the hall.

"Let's go early to practice. We'll kick some balls around," said Mia and Amarjeet, dragging me back to their table. "Can you make it, Cat? You played great yesterday."

"Sure," I promised, even though I had no idea how I'd get to practice early. Mom was working late and had told me to pick up Sookie from school by three and take her to swimming lessons. Then I thought of my neighbor, Jasper.

My teacher didn't even look up from her desk when I sneaked out of math early, and once I was in the hall, another teacher didn't ask where I was supposed to be. When I bumped into Ms. Sevren, she only smiled and waved at me. *People at school must really be looking forward to the big game.* Maybe they assumed anything I was doing was related to soccer business and that was okay.

Once I found Jasper's class, I waited outside the door until the bell rang.

"Jasper, can you – " He didn't let me finish.

"Hi, Cat. Are we still on for the big Monopoly game at your place next Friday night?" Jasper asked as he pushed his glasses up on his nose.

Jasper had hung out at our house a few Friday nights when his parents worked at their restaurant. But that would have to change.

"Maybe I won't be able to make it." I felt a twinge of guilt when I saw the disappointment on Jasper's face. "With soccer, I'm pretty busy now ..." I said vaguely, before asking, "Hey, could you pick up Sookie for me and take her to swimming lessons from now on – just when I have practice?" What I was asking Jasper was huge, the kind of thing you asked a best friend. But I hoped he didn't think that's what he was to me. I just didn't know anyone else well enough yet.

"Um, well, I've got my paper route." This time Jasper pushed his glasses all the way on top of his spiked black hair. "I guess I could drop her off, but I can't wait for her because I have to deliver papers. Maybe I could pick her up when I'm finished."

Not ideal, but maybe it would be okay. "After you pick her up, could you then drop her off at Grimoire's soccer field?"

"Okay," he said. "But about that Friday night, my parents were sort of expecting – "

"Cat, are you coming?" Amarjeet and Mia were waiting for me at the end of the hall.

"Sorry, got to go." I flung my bag on my shoulder and raced after them.

When we ran past the Emporium, Mr. Keating was waiting under the striped awning. He signaled for us to stop. I thought he was going to ask me what I'd been up to the other day. Instead, he went over to the apple barrel and plucked three of the biggest apples and polished them on his apron.

He held one out to me; it gleamed as red as his cheeks. "For the soccer player. You'll need your strength," he said.

Being in the soccer match was like being a celebrity. Before I bit into the juicy apple, I thanked him. Then he handed out the other apples. Crunching our fruit, we all walked down the main street as storekeepers and shoppers smiled and waved. Even dogs came up and wagged their tails when we passed their houses.

As the three of us climbed Grim Hill, it

appeared that the fog, which had hung over the hill all day, was rolling back, out of our way. Once we got to the top of the hill and onto the soccer field, the sky cleared. I sat down on the bleachers and slipped into my soccer boots. They pinched my feet, reminding me that they were too tight. To make things worse, a blister had bubbled up on my toe from yesterday, making me limp onto the soccer field.

"Well aren't you a sorry-looking player," said Ms. Sinster, my coach. "What's wrong with your foot?"

"I have a blister." There was no point adding that it was because my boots were too tight. I never even mentioned that to Mom because I knew there was no money in this month's budget for new boots. Maybe there'd be some spare cash when the big soccer match was closer. My coach handed me a couple of bandages and bustled off to organize the other girls on the team.

At first we all stumbled around as we started the practice. But slowly, it was as if I got hooked up to that amplifier again. There really was music pouring out of Grimoire School; I figured that there must be an orchestra rehearsal at the same time we practiced. The energizing music and golden sunshine seeped in, making me feel good – light, and springy, as if I could run and jump for hours. The sound of wind whistling through the woods hummed in my ears.

Grimoire School was singing a song. I couldn't make out the words, but I loved the melody. My foot stopped hurting and my focus improved – and so did my soccer moves. I landed all my shots, dribbled the ball on the field, and passed perfectly. Mia and Amarjeet were really good players too.

The game swooped over me like a giant wave, with me floating on top as everything else was blocked out. The whole world slipped away and nothing else mattered. Well, not quite. This time I didn't get so carried away that I forgot about Sookie. Like clockwork, at exactly four, Jasper delivered her to the bleachers.

She didn't look happy.

CHAPTER 5

A Dangerous Juggling Act

SOOKIE'S BLOND HAIR was still wet from swimming and was plastered to her skull. She sat huddled on the bench, frowning deeply, with her arms folded in front of her as she glared at me.

Tough, I thought. She'd have to wait until soccer practice finished before I could go over and see what was bugging her.

The ball sailed toward me, and I head-butted it past the goalie and into the goal. The other girls cheered. I could get used to this.

After practice, the coach gathered us into a group. "We don't have much time before the soccer match. There's a lot at stake, so we have to work as hard as we can. Practice will be every day after school until five. On Saturdays and Sundays, we'll practice from ten in the morning until three in the afternoon."

Wow. It's not that I didn't love being here, because I did. But this practice schedule didn't leave much time for homework *or* babysitting little sisters. I was about to mention that to Ms. Sinster, but Amarjeet spoke up first.

"My mom won't let me skip Punjabi school,"

she said to the coach.

"Yes she will," said Ms. Sinster.

Amarjeet appeared doubtful.

"I'm a bridesmaid for my sister's wedding," said Mia. "I can't miss the shower, or rehearsal, or dress fittings."

"You can now," said the coach.

Another girl mentioned that she had music lessons every Saturday.

"You won't anymore," Ms. Sinster said and smiled the same nasty smile as the witch on the Grimoire soccer poster.

I couldn't offer any decent explanation for my sudden feeling of dread. Maybe it was Ms. Sinster's face and the way her gray eyes looked down her long nose – it was as if I could feel the iciness of her stare stabbing into me. Not only did I believe those girls wouldn't miss a single practice, but a cold chill crept up my spine. The last thing I thought I should mention was that I had to take care of my little sister sometimes.

"Are there any other complaints?" The coach glared at me.

Keeping my lips sealed, I shook my head no, just like the other girls. Ms. Sinster dismissed us and I ran toward the bleachers. Now it was time to face the music and see what was up with my sister.

I was right. Sookie was furious. At first, she barely talked to me as we walked down Grim Hill.

"So you're mad at me because I had Jasper pick you up."

"No," she barely grunted.

I didn't think that would be it because she adored Jasper. "Are you mad that we didn't go for frozen yogurt after swimming, like we used to?"

"No." This time she snorted.

"You hate waiting for me at the soccer field," I said.

She contemplated that for a minute, and then she scowled.

"I don't like this place at all," Sookie answered as she looked up at the school. "And sometimes waiting for you will get boring, I'm sure."

Only sometimes? Sookie would *never* like hanging around up here. And it was only going to get worse because she would practically have to live up here until after the soccer match.

"But that's not the problem," she finished.

"Then what's the matter?" I almost shouted, which wouldn't have been smart. The last thing I needed was for her to stay mad at me and tell Mom that I had Jasper pick her up. Sookie was my responsibility, not Jasper's. "Really, Sookie, what's the matter?" I asked coaxingly this time.

"You told Jasper you probably couldn't play Monopoly with us next Friday night," she finally admitted. "If you're not there, he won't play with just me." Sookie finished with a *harrumph*, folded her arms again, and stamped her foot.

Aha. That's what was wrong. Well, maybe it would be wise to stay on the good side of both Sookie *and* Jasper, considering I'd have to foist Sookie on Jasper quite a bit. There wouldn't be a lot of time left over from soccer, especially for babysitting.

"Look," I said, "I won't change the plan. Next Friday night is still on."

Sookie nodded solemnly. Peace was restored.

As we walked down the hill, the fog hung in clots, almost like cotton batting caught in the tree branches. But when we moved toward the strange mist, we never quite met up with it. The fog danced away. While Sookie and I made a sport of chasing the fog, I kept reasoning that I was really being fair about all this. Sookie would hate being stuck with me all the time while I concentrated on soccer, and I was grateful for any help Jasper could provide. But underneath, a darker side of me knew that I wanted to stay focused on one thing and one thing only – my game. If that meant inviting Jasper over once in a while in order to entertain Sookie, that was the price I had to pay.

* * *

The next two weeks went by quickly with hardly a spare moment. And when there was one, I had a ton of new friends to spend it with.

When Friday morning rolled around, Amarjeet and Mia were waiting for me at my locker.

"You weren't online last night, Cat," they complained.

Sookie had hogged the computer to do a project on ants and bees. Instead of mentioning that, I asked, "What's up?"

"We're going to meet at the Bubble Tea Palace tonight. Our whole team is going so that we can make game plans for the big match," explained Amarjeet. Then she said with absolute despair, "I should really enjoy these last moments because I might not be on the team much longer if I have to miss Saturday practice. The coach is getting angry."

"Don't worry, it'll probably all work out. And you *will* enjoy yourself," Mia said, patting Amarjeet's shoulder. "By coincidence, some of the guys, like Zach and Mitch, are supposed to show up later."

Amarjeet shot her an "only soccer matters" look, but I could tell she was a bit more cheerful after hearing that news.

As I stood there listening to my friends, I began to get another sinking feeling. Amarjeet was a top player, and she increased our chances of winning. Our team couldn't lose her. To make things worse, I had to skip a great night out working on game plans so that I could play Monopoly with my little sister and a boy a whole year younger than me. *Great*. How was I going to juggle all of these balls in the air – friends, coach, Sookie, *and* Jasper – and most importantly, not let anything interfere with what really mattered: winning the scholarship?

CHAPTER 6

Whispers from the Past

THAT EVENING, I consoled myself about my boring night in by trying on my soccer uniform for about the twelfth time. I stood in front of the full-length mirror. The ragged hemmed skort and black and green socks seemed perfect for a Halloween soccer match. I loved Halloween. Dad had always called me his "October girl." He used to say that my hair was as dark and shiny as the autumn chestnuts that fell from the trees. My eyes, he joked, were "Cat's eye green." Since the divorce, I have really missed having him around.

The doorbell rang, interrupting my thoughts.

"Cat!" Mom called from downstairs. "Your friend Jasper's here."

At the word "friend," I gritted my teeth. He was a *neighbor*, not a friend. Jasper wasn't a bit like the popular kids I used to hang around with at my old school, or like the kids I'd started hanging out with at Darkmont. Still, Jasper was really smart. He was a reading addict and could talk about any book, so he was pretty interesting, too. And *he* thought I was his friend.

"Cat!" Mom called again. She shouldn't have

bothered because Sookie had already appeared behind me in the mirror, tugging my arm and pointing downstairs. Unlike me, Sookie thought Jasper was the best thing ever.

"Hurry," she pleaded. She danced excitedly, and her short blond hair – which was straight and shiny like Dad's, but blond like Mom's – bobbed like a halo of light. I understood why Dad used to call her his "Sunshine girl."

"Coming, Mom." I reluctantly started tugging off my socks. "Isn't this uniform great?" I asked Sookie.

She shrugged. "Not really," she said quietly. "The black looks gloomy, just like the school. C'mon," she said louder this time. "Jasper is waiting, and Mom said he could join us for dinner." Then she vanished downstairs.

What was up with Sookie? She usually went crazy over any piece of clothing that belonged to me. And I would have let her try on the socks. Carefully I folded my awesome uniform, went downstairs, and greeted our guest.

In the kitchen, chili bubbled in the cast iron pot. I could smell peppers and spice. Mom had made taco salad, our favorite, to go with the chili. The smell of cinnamon trailed out of the oven – apple pie! The table was already set with company placemats for Jasper – which gave me a pinch of guilt. Usually, I came home from school and cut up the vegetables for dinner. But between soccer practice and modeling my new uniform, I'd forgotten. Sookie hadn't set the table either. Instead, she was already sitting down and babbling to Jasper while Mom arranged the napkins. Even though Mom looked tired, she had gone all out. After helping put food on each plate, I slumped down into my chair and started eating. Between heaping mouthfuls, I thanked Mom for the great dinner.

Mom smiled. She was trying hard to make it up to us because of the divorce and the move. She said she really wanted Sookie and me to adjust. I think that meant make friends, be happy with our new home, and mostly, not miss Dad too much. We had hardly ever seen our father before the divorce. When they were married, he was always away for work. What I really missed was looking forward to when he'd come home. I sighed. All summer I had wanted to be happier for Mom, but it had been hard.

"Payday was yesterday, so even though it's overdue, I thought this dinner could be a celebration of you making the team," Mom said to me. "By the way, Cat, how is everything going these days?"

"Not bad," I said. My fork stopped halfway to my mouth in surprise. This was the first time I realized how much everything had changed.

School had started out horribly and only got worse until the soccer tryouts. It was as if soccer made my life bearable, and the fact that a scholarship was just around the corner made things better than all right.

Mom relaxed a bit and started eating. "Good. Beginning a new school at your age can be difficult, so I'm glad it's going well. Although, I really wish you could go to Grimoire School," Mom mentioned. "But the tuition is extremely expensive, and even with staff discounts, I just can't afford it. The soccer match is critical. It makes all the difference for your future."

What happened to Mom's usual saying, "Don't put all your eggs in one basket?" She suddenly sounded as if my team *had* to win the scholarship.

"You need to check out how strong the Ghosts are," offered Jasper. "We should watch them practice."

"Really work on your kick shot, Cat," said Mom. "That's your strong point."

Sookie stared at Mom and frowned. "I don't see what the big deal is." She shook her head. "Cat shouldn't get so caught up in this, right Mom?"

Oddly ignoring Sookie, Mom said to me, "You have a fifty-fifty chance at the scholarship. You've got to put everything you have into it, Cat. Everything." Her eyes shone.

Mom never pressured me about sports, but at least if she was this supportive, she wouldn't mind me doing less homework – which meant I could be free for lots of soccer practices.

The phone rang, and Mom got up to answer it after telling Sookie to sit back down and eat.

When we heard, "I'm glad no one was hurt," our heads snapped in Mom's direction.

"Who was that?" I asked as soon as she hung up.

"Mrs. Singh," she said. "Apparently there was a fire and Amarjeet's Punjabi school burned down. Since it will be months before it's rebuilt, she wanted me to mention it to Ms. Sinster, your coach, when I see her at work. Apparently there had been some kind of conflict with soccer practice."

A prickly feeling crawled up my neck – it was as if a plump spider had landed on me. But I brushed the sensation away. I knew Amarjeet would be glad not to have to miss soccer now.

"We really needed Amarjeet on the team," I told them, feeling relieved. "Now there's an even better chance at winning the scholarship."

Only Sookie didn't seem excited for me. She squirmed, even through dessert. Before we'd finished, she jumped out of her chair.

"Mom, can we set the game up in the attic?" Sookie asked. We liked hanging out in the attic because Mom never bugged us about keeping that area of the house tidy. But she also liked to work up there when she didn't want to be disturbed.

Mom nodded and said, "Fine, just don't touch the files on the desk."

Jasper and I started clearing the table. "Why don't you and Sookie go get started," I told him. "I'll dry the dishes." It was the most helpful thing Jasper could do at the moment. Sookie was in such a rush to clear the table, she almost dropped a stack of plates – she was too impatient to carry them one by one.

Mom filled the sink with steaming hot water and globs of dish soap, but when I grabbed a fresh striped tea towel out of the drawer, she ushered me to the stairs.

"Go on," she said. "I'll finish." Mom grabbed a greasy pan. "Have fun with your friend."

"He's not actually my ..." I started to say, but I didn't finish. To be fair about Jasper, over the summer he was the only other kid I'd met. Before the soccer tryouts, it wasn't as if other kids in my new town had been lining up to be friends with me. I'd hung out at the swimming pool and at the baseball park, but I couldn't seem to click with anyone. It was hard to believe that last year a really cute boy had asked me to the school dance. How low I'd sunk. That is, until I'd made the team. But it didn't seem right to turn my back on Jasper now, even if he was younger and not considered cool.

So instead of finishing my sentence about him not being my friend, I nodded, then climbed the wood stairs up past the bedrooms and to the third-floor attic.

Stepping through the skinny doorway at the top of the stairs, I had to duck under the slanted ceiling until I stood in the middle of the attic. Old yellow wallpaper with faded red roses covered the walls, and peeling green linoleum covered the floor. The place practically shouted, "Come in and have fun – don't worry about making a mess." An old trunk sat in a corner, and one day soon I hoped to figure out how to open it without breaking it. A spooky, headless sewing dummy stuck with pins stood by the window – just the finishing touch to this awesome, creepy place.

Jasper was sitting by the dust-covered window reading some old notebook he'd found. Sookie looked angry. "We haven't even taken the game out yet," she said and gave Jasper a little push. "He won't stop reading."

"I found this journal by the Monopoly game," he mumbled.

Jasper was the kind of reading addict who probably read the backs of cereal boxes. "C'mon Jasper," I said. "Sookie wants to play the game."

When he shoved the journal under my nose, I saw that it belonged to someone named Alice

Greystone. Flipping to an entry, I read that Alice got the journal for her ninth birthday. Her writing was spidery, as if it were written with those old-fashioned pens that you had to dip in an inkwell. The page began *October 13th* – around seventy years ago. I began reading out loud:

Since my sister joined the Witches soccer team, she never plays with me anymore, wrote Alice Greystone. *All Lucinda talks about is her bothersome Halloween soccer match. I don't want to wait for her at that school on Grim Hill. I don't like it there. It feels wrong.*

It struck me that if Sookie had a diary, she'd write almost the same words! Surprised, I glanced up at her, thinking I understood better why she hated hanging around the practice field and why she didn't like my uniform. Sookie missed spending time with me.

Feeling guilty, I started to close the journal. "We'd better set up the game," I said quietly. But Jasper grabbed it, flipped a few pages forward, and handed it back to me.

"Look," he said, pushing his glasses up on his nose. I began to read:

October 30 – Tomorrow is Halloween, the day of the big game. The whole town is going. All everyone can talk about is if the Witches or Ghosts are going to win. The winners get a scholarship to Grimoire School. I can't wait for it all to be over. I keep having a bad feeling about the game, but Lucinda won't listen to me. She even tells Mother she's watching me, but she sneaks off and plays soccer with her team. She never used to lie. I hope she is nice again when the game is over.

The attic suddenly felt cold.

"So there was another Halloween soccer match about seventy years ago with the same first prize – weird," I said. "Did Lucinda's team win?"

Jasper shrugged, leaned over my shoulder, and flipped one page ahead.

November 1, Alice had written. *I was picked to sing in the school concert. Mother was pleased.*

"But who won the game? Did her sister get the scholarship to Grimoire?" I asked again, flipping more pages, stopping, and reading more sections to Jasper and Sookie.

November 14, I had a lovely birthday dinner with Mother, Father, Auntie Jane, and cousin Mary.

"Who cares?" Sookie shouted impatiently.

She had a point. Whoever won seventy years ago had nothing to do with us right now. I tossed the journal on the desk. Jasper took one longing glance at the journal before setting up the Monopoly game.

We dealt out our Monopoly money and once we rolled the dice, the journal entries we'd read slipped back into the past where they belonged.

But later that night, after Jasper left, and as

Sookie snored softly in her room, I lay in bed wondering about the journal. *Why hadn't Alice mentioned who won the big game?*

Something else was odd about that journal, but I couldn't quite put my finger on it.

CHAPTER 7

The Price of Team Spirit

ON MONDAY AFTER school, Jasper met me at my locker.

"Cat," Jasper said as he pushed his glasses up on his head. He seemed worried. "I've been trying to reach you all weekend. You're never around."

"Sorry – soccer practice," I explained quickly. "What's up?"

"About that journal we had found – you know, I got curious about who won the match that Alice's sister played in long ago. Accessing old headlines online should have been easy, but I couldn't find anything. So I went to the library and found computer disks that have archives of the town newspaper." Glancing over his shoulder, Jasper then whispered, "When I looked up the dates from Alice's journal, I noticed a very peculiar thing about that original soccer game – "

"Cat," Mia said, cutting Jasper short as she approached with Amarjeet following behind her, "we have to hurry, or we'll be late for practice."

"Oh right, and I have to stop at my house first to get extra bandages," I said, wincing at the thought of stuffing my aching toes into those tiny soccer boots yet again. Even though it seemed interesting, Jasper and his journal news would have to wait.

"How do you play so well with such sore feet anyway?" asked Amarjeet.

"That's right, you scored *three* goals yesterday," said Mia, shaking her head in amazement.

"Um, Cat..."Jasper said quietly. "Maybe we could meet after practice and talk. I could stay for a few minutes after I drop off Sookie and –"

Mia and Amarjeet ignored him as they escorted me down the hall and out the door.

"Maybe!" I called back.

The three of us hurried to my house, and my friends followed me inside when I went in to grab the bandages. An Emporium shopping bag sat on the dining room table. Mom had attached a note to it.

You might need these, the note said, but before I could read any further, I had to rip open the bag.

Inside was a pair of new soccer boots! They were super deluxe, black with stripes that were the same witch-green color of my jersey and socks. The leather was as soft as butter; these boots must have cost a fortune.

I dug them out of the box and when I slipped them on, it was foot heaven. "They are perfect," I told my friends as I read the rest of Mom's note.

Mr. Keating pointed them out to me as I walked

by his store during my lunch hour. I couldn't resist, and it was as if the idea of new boots popped into both our heads at the same time. Why I didn't think of them before, I don't know. After all, this soccer match is everything, she wrote.

Funny, that was something I should be saying. Coming from my mother, it sounded slightly off. Still, I scooped up my new boots and the three of us headed up Grim Hill to soccer practice.

"The fog always seems to dance just ahead of us," said Mia as we climbed to the top of the hill.

"Just like a mirage," observed Amarjeet. "The same as when you see a puddle of water ahead of you on the road, but when you get close, it disappears."

"But it isn't a mirage," I pointed out. "At night the fog rolls all the way down the hill and covers the whole town." Before bed I look out my bedroom window into what Mom calls pea soup. "By morning, though, the sun is always shining."

"And," said Mia, "even though there is always fog drifting around up here, there is never any fog on the soccer fields during practice."

The three of us turned and said, "Nothing seems to get in the way of soccer." That we'd all said it at the same time struck us as funny and we laughed, racing onto the soccer field.

We enjoyed every moment of the practice. Just as we were finishing up, Jasper swung by with

Sookie. "Hey Cat, I was trying to tell you earlier that there was something not right about – " he began.

Mia and Amarjeet pulled me away from him. Sookie stood between the four of us, clearly annoyed.

Mia said, "Some of the girls are going to the soccer field on the other side of the hill so they can spy on the Ghosts." Smirking, she then said, "Come on, Cat. This is important espionage."

Amarjeet giggled.

"What's so funny?" I asked.

"You might find spying on the people sitting in the bleachers a lot more interesting than whatever the Ghosts are up to," hinted Mia.

"You could come," I said lamely to Jasper. Sookie looked up at him hopefully.

"No. I'd better go." He shook his head. "My parents expect me back by now."

"What about me?" Sookie complained.

"Don't you want to hang out with the big kids?" I asked.

Sookie didn't look eager. I held my breath, hoping she wouldn't kick up a fuss and praying that Jasper might offer a reprieve and take her off my hands. Neither of those things happened. Finally, when she saw there weren't any real choices, she took my hand.

We went to the soccer field on the other side of Grimoire School. Many more trees surrounded this field, casting shadows over the ground. Zipping up my jacket against a chilly wind that seemed to only blow over this area, I elbowed Mia. "Hey," I said, "aren't you supposed to be shopping with your sister for bridesmaids' dresses this afternoon?"

"I forgot to tell you – my sister broke up with her fiancé," whispered Mia. "The wedding's been canceled. She won't stop crying." Mia shrugged her shoulders. "Now I won't miss any practices."

Nothing really did get in the way of soccer, I thought. Then, hearing voices on the bleacher in front of us, I finally figured out why Mia and Amarjeet were *so* interested in spying on the Ghosts, and it had nothing to do with the team's soccer technique. The cute guys from Darkmont had come to watch this practice – we were sitting behind Zach and his friends!

Mia discreetly pointed to one of them, whispering, "Mitch is Darkmont's star basketball player." Her eyes sparkled with admiration.

"I'm getting a drink of water," Sookie told me, sounding more than a little bored.

Sookie wandered off and I settled in, watching the practice. It was strangely fascinating. The Ghosts ran wildly across the field, stumbling over the ball, missing obvious shots, and no one could score, even though there wasn't even a goalie.

I didn't get it – Darkmont had no soccer team, so the tryouts had a huge pool of the best athletes in town. How could these girls be so bad?

"This field is dark, and the shadows keep getting in the way of the ball," Amarjeet reasoned.

So she noticed too, how it felt wrong – different – on this side of the school. The air smelled harsh and moldy, and the melodic music I always heard coming out of the school during practice was out of tune and jarring on this side. But that was only part of the problem. "These players don't have any real sense of the game," I observed.

"That's because Cindy says the school wants you and your friends," Sookie interjected after wandering back to the bleachers. "You and your friends *want* to win more, and the school needs that kind of energy." Sookie frowned and her face grew darker. In a worried voice she said, "But you can't let that happen. You can't win, *no one can.* Cindy would tell you that herself, but you don't see her as well as I do. So she says you wouldn't hear her very clearly either."

I had no idea what she was talking about. *Cindy*, that's what Sookie had called that weird Goth girl back at the tryouts. Scanning the field, I said, "I don't see her here, so exactly when were you talking to her?"

"Just now," Sookie said. "And at some of the other practices after Jasper dropped me off." Sookie got a sly smile. "You don't see everything up here on the hill. You hardly even notice me."

All the hairs stood up on the back of my neck. I really needed to keep a closer eye on my sister. That Goth girl was a bit too creepy, and I wanted Sookie to stay away from her.

"Don't go off talking with anyone unless you check with me first," I warned her. Sookie got her stubborn look. "Cindy told me she never comes out to talk to people. But I look a lot like her sister, so the first time we met, she'd come to see if I was her." Sookie smiled. "Now she visits me almost every time I'm up here. She likes me. I'll ask her more questions about the school if you want."

"Don't ask her anything without me," I demanded. I should have said it a lot louder, but then Emily from the Ghosts stumbled and made a horrible shot.

If the Ghosts kept playing like this, we were sure to win the scholarship.

As long as nothing else interfered with our practices.

CHAPTER 8

A Sinister Warning

AS THE NEXT weeks flew by, I couldn't get enough of soccer. So when the coach scheduled an extra practice early Saturday morning, I woke up with lots of energy, eager to get on the field. I'd been having the same dream every night about winning the match and getting the coveted scholarship to Grimoire School.

After I dressed, I slipped on my shin pads, socks, and my totally cool soccer boots. They felt squishy and soft. My game had improved even more because of them.

Mom and Sookie were still asleep when I made my way to the kitchen, which was a first for me. After I'd finished a bowl of cereal and was about to leave, Mom came downstairs rubbing her eyes and yawning – but she was dressed in a skirt and sweater instead of her Saturday jeans.

"I've been called into work today, so you'll need to take care of Sookie," Mom said.

The red kitchen clock above the sink said quarter to eight. Sookie was a slowpoke, so I'd never get to practice in time.

"But I'll be late." Worry crept into my voice as I

pictured the coach's eyes, as gray and cold as a gravestone. My skin prickled with goose bumps.

"Sorry. I didn't know you had to get to practice so early or I'd have mentioned it last night." Mom grabbed her purse and left quickly out the front door. I scrambled upstairs – this wasn't going to be easy.

Just as I thought, I had to drag Sookie kicking and screaming out from under her patchwork quilt.

"You can pick out any movie you want for tonight." I never let her choose, but I'd promise her anything and everything if she'd hurry right now.

"No." She wasn't even tempted.

"You can wear whatever you want from my closet." That was hard for me to offer, but she didn't care. She just shook her head.

"Do you want cookies for breakfast? What about three extra dollars from my allowance," I bargained, but nothing worked.

"It's cold outside and I want to watch cartoons. I don't want to go!" Sookie hollered. "You can't make me."

"If you don't get up, I won't ever play cards or Monopoly with you again." Okay, I'm not proud, but I threatened her. "And if you don't hurry, I'm never inviting Jasper here again."

I expected her to say she'd tell Mom. She didn't. Instead her eyes got kind of watery, but then she pulled on her jacket over her pajama top. She tugged on a pair of jogging pants that she dug out of her clothes hamper. She didn't even ask me to help her brush her hair. For a few short moments, Sookie was eerily silent, and I almost believed she had become more cooperative – until, that is, she came out of the house behind me, slamming the door so loud, it echoed down the street.

Sookie sullenly trudged up Grim Hill next to me. Her angry breaths turned to white puffs in the chilly morning air. It was as if she had steam coming out of her nose and mouth. As she crunched dry cornflakes that I'd dumped in a plastic cup for her breakfast, I heard her sniff a lot.

I don't know what got into me, but I snapped. "Don't be such a baby and hurry up!" Honestly, if I wasn't afraid to be late, I would have never been so mean to her. The guilt twisted in my stomach. Maybe I'd take her with me to meet Jasper this afternoon. He'd been bugging me again lately, saying that we had to talk about the journal. My stomach tightened another notch because I'd gone out of my way to avoid him, making sure I ducked out of school early with Mia and Amarjeet before the last school bell. I didn't have time for anything but soccer – didn't he and Sookie get that?

My guilt didn't evaporate. *Fine.* I'd blow the last of my allowance on pizza for us. Maybe we could go to a park. It was about time Sookie made some friends her own age – not that she ever had time to socialize. She was always stuck coming to soccer with me.

Despite bullying Sookie, I was still fifteen minutes late for practice. She sat in a miserable heap on the bleachers while I ran off to do laps and catch up with Amarjeet and Mia.

"Did you hear about Emily, the girl on the Ghosts?" asked Amarjeet. "Her dad didn't want her to play in the soccer practices on the weekend when she was supposed to be visiting him. Well, he suddenly got transferred up north, and now her parents are having a big custody battle. Emily's not allowed any more visits with him."

The three of us looked at each other, but this time we didn't laugh. Instead we said nervously, "Well, at least she can play soccer."

As I ran around the field, I thought about Emily and her dad, Amarjeet's smoldering school, and Mia's broken-hearted sister – all the coincidences made my heart thump even harder. It wasn't just as if nothing was going to get in the way of the scholarship match – it was more ominous than that. It was as if *no one got in the way of soccer*.

Caught up in my whirlwind thoughts, I'd stopped in mid stride, so it was a second before I noticed that everyone had begun stumbling as they ran laps. Sookie had chosen this time to revenge the bad way I'd treated her. She'd started kicking soccer balls at us as we ran, and she knocked over all the water bottles, tossing them onto the field and into everyone's way.

Before I could stop her, she took all of our jackets and piled them in front of the goal posts. The coach walked toward her purposefully. A worry hit me like a punch in the gut. What if Sookie became a distraction at practice? Distractions had a way of being eliminated around here. I ran toward her.

By the time I reached Sookie and the coach, all I heard was Ms. Sinster softly say, "Now sit up on the bench and wait patiently for your sister."

Sure, that sounded innocent, but there was something about her tone of voice that made me feel as if the gates of hell would open up if Sookie didn't do as she was told. It was enough to make stubborn Sookie nod meekly, march over to the bench, and sit down.

Warily, I returned to practice, keeping one eye on the soccer ball and the other eye on Sookie. She didn't budge until we got a quick lunch break. I brought her some orange slices and half the egg sandwich I'd packed for myself – I hadn't had time to pack her a proper lunch. When I went back on the field, Sookie took one look at Ms. Sinster and sat back down on the bench.

Once I started chasing the ball again, I kept checking on Sookie, even when Mia elbowed me during a time-out and pointed to the bleachers. Some of the guys from Darkmont had come to watch us. Mia smiled up at Mitch. Golden-haired, green-eyed Zach waved at *me*. I waved back. Sookie glared at me the whole time they were there, and for a while after they left. But she sat quietly on the bench until practice finished. She didn't start complaining until we were getting ready to leave.

"I hate it here. This place is bad. I'm not going to come with you anymore. You'd better quit the team."

Because the coach was close by, I wanted Sookie to keep quiet.

"Stop complaining and I'll buy you pizza *and* take you to the park," I said.

"Cindy said that you wouldn't listen to my warning," Sookie snorted.

When Sookie mentioned Cindy's name, Ms. Sinster's head snapped up, and she moved in the direction of where we were sitting on the lowest bleacher.

The coach approached us as I nervously wondered how Sookie had managed to escape my radar again after she'd caused trouble. Quickly I whispered, "When was that weird Goth girl here?"

"Just now," Sookie said smugly. "Guess you don't know everything."

The coach came closer to us. Her long, straight

black hair swung against her shoulders.

"Oh," Sookie continued, "and Cindy says to remind you that you'd better not win the soccer game. She says – "

Ms. Sinster raised a claw-like hand toward Sookie as she approached us.

"Shut up!" I told Sookie.

CHAPTER 9

A Diabolical Distraction

SOOKIE STOPPED HER excited babble and looked up at me in amazement. "What?"

Ms. Sinster stood in front of us. "Great playing, Cat," was all she said.

I sighed in relief. The way she'd been moving toward us had given me a horrible feeling. Most likely, I was overreacting and my uneasiness was all in my head. This was no time for my imagination to go into overdrive. I had to keep my focus, and my coach, who didn't exactly ooze praise, had just said, "Great playing!" I floated all the way home on those words.

It wasn't until we got up to the front steps that Sookie reminded me that I'd promised we would get together with Jasper that afternoon. Automatically, I began to brush her off, but I hesitated because now that I was away from the practice field, an uneasiness crept up my spine again. This time, I didn't ignore it. What if there *was* something to Sookie's close call with the coach and the disturbing things she kept telling me about her new friend? Maybe it was time to face the fact that Jasper was noticing other odd stuff and that I'd gotten seriously sidetracked. "Yes," I said. "Let's call Jasper."

Before I could even finish the sentence, Sookie shot off the porch and ran across the yard to get Jasper. A couple of minutes later, she and Jasper walked up our front pathway. I sent Sookie in to grab us some juice, and I quickly told Jasper everything – about the strange coincidences that happened to the other girls on my team and how nothing got in the way of practice.

"And after we were late for practice, Sookie kicked up such a fuss, I thought the coach would do something to her." I stopped and thought about it for a second. "I have no idea what. And I can't explain it because the coach didn't even yell at Sookie. But I never felt so scared in my life. It all seems …" I trailed off, feeling foolish.

"… diabolical," Sookie said, sneaking up behind us. She handed us both a juice box.

Where did she learn a word like that?

Before I had a chance to respond, the phone rang and she ran to answer it. She always wanted to be the one to answer the phone.

Jasper didn't laugh or even smile at the curious worries I'd told him about. Instead he said, "I've been trying to tell you that there's something bizarre about all of this. Those old newspapers I'd looked up on the computer at the library had made a huge deal about the upcoming soccer match." Then he got an odd look on his face. "But after Halloween, when the match was over, the local paper never even mentioned which team won the game."

What Jasper was saying seemed vaguely familiar. "There was something like that in the old journal we found upstairs," I said. "It didn't mention who won, but did it ever mention if her sister got the scholarship? Maybe the answer is right there in that journal."

"Yeah," said Jasper, looking a bit startled. "That's a good idea. We *should* take a closer look."

Sookie got off the phone. "Mom will be home soon. She's stopping at the Emporium," she said from the front doorway.

Jasper and I went inside and climbed up the stairs to the attic. Of course, Sookie insisted on joining us.

"Are we going to play Monopoly again?" Sookie asked, her voice brimming with hope.

"No, we're looking for that old journal we found before."

"Alice's journal? How come?" Sookie sounded disappointed but curious.

At least *she* remembered the girl's name. All of it seemed kind of foggy in my brain. "We just want to take a closer look at it," I said, ducking through the low door and stepping into the attic. "Do you have any idea where we left it?"

"We tossed it on the table." Jasper crossed the floor and started shuffling game boxes around. "Or maybe we threw it on the desk."

The three of us quickly investigated – no journal. Then we checked the bookshelves, behind the battered old trunk, and under the table we had used to play Monopoly.

"Did we dream the journal up?" I wondered out loud.

"The three of us? Not likely," snorted Sookie. She always was the logical one.

"It's got to be here somewhere," Jasper said, wiping the lenses of his glasses clean and jamming them on his face as if they'd give him X-ray vision.

"So what? It's not here. Who cares, anyway?" Sookie was getting bored. She just happened to have brought out the Monopoly game.

"We wanted to see who won the scholarship," Jasper said. "We couldn't find that information before, remember?"

"Not really," muttered Sookie. "I didn't really pay attention. If you're so curious about who won the stupid match, maybe I could ask Cindy. She seems to know a lot about Grimoire."

"Not unless I'm with you," I said slowly. "I don't want you talking to that *Cindy*. It's not cool that she hides when I'm around."

"She doesn't hide." Sookie sounded surprised. "You just don't look very carefully."

For a second, I felt guilty again. I knew I should have been better about keeping a close eye on her. But then Jasper said to Sookie, "I've dropped you off at the soccer field lots of times, and I've never seen that girl either."

"Do you want me to ask her or not?" Sookie demanded.

"I'd feel better if you left her out of this," I said.

Sookie set her jaw in her all too stubborn way. Then she stuck her tongue out at me. Promising myself I'd pay even more attention to her the next time we were on the soccer field, I slid down on top of the trunk and sat, thinking. Jasper kept fiddling with his glasses. Sookie stared longingly at the Monopoly game.

"You know," Jasper finally said, "the journal and the newspaper at the library archives are probably not the only source of information about that Halloween game back then. Maybe there are other documents in the library's online records."

"Right." I nodded. Before, I didn't want to know anything about that first soccer game, but now I felt I had to find out who won that match, the Witches or the Ghosts. "The game should be mentioned somewhere else, but I assume you did a search?"

Jasper said, "Well, I could recheck the entire database again and maybe expand my search."

"That's a plan then. We'll expand our search.

Maybe – "

The door slammed downstairs and I heard my mother.

"Cat, come down quickly," she called. "I want to talk to you."

We ran downstairs. Jasper said hi to my mom and slipped out the front door, before saying we should meet up soon. Sookie waved goodbye to him, but I only waved halfheartedly because I was too busy staring at the Emporium shopping bags Mom had put on the table.

"I was thinking – why don't you throw a big Halloween party next Saturday?" Mom said. "I know it'll be a week before Halloween, but this way your party won't get in the way of the soccer game. Invite as many people as you like, boys included."

This was my mom? She'd let me have a party? With boys? All last year she told me I was too young for boy-girl parties. I got that excited feeling in my stomach. Maybe Zach would come.

Mom started pulling out decorations from the bag: expensive Halloween pumpkin lights, a large plastic jack-o'-lantern, black and orange crepe paper, packages of balloons, and weird sticky stuff to make fake cobwebs. When she hauled out fancy paper plates, napkins, and cups decorated with witches and ghosts, I couldn't believe it – all of it must have cost a fortune.

"I don't know what came over me. I couldn't

resist," Mom said.

At that point, my worries about the coach, the coincidences of the other girls, and the disappearing journal, all evaporated.

Wasn't I having the best time of my life, not to mention getting closer to the scholarship? As long as I kept a closer eye on Sookie and made sure she wasn't causing any trouble – that was all that mattered.

I couldn't wait for my party.

CHAPTER 10

A Grave Oversight

BECAUSE I WANTED to keep my extraordinary luck going, when Jasper met up with me on Monday, nattering about how I'd promised to help him research the soccer match, I wasn't into it anymore. Sure, up in the spooky attic after my scare with Sookie and the coach, anything seemed possible. But in the daylight, with my other friends waiting for me at my locker, I got impatient. Couldn't he get over the fact that he wasn't going to be able to find out anything about the results of the big Halloween match long ago?

"The whole town seemed to forget about which team won," said Jasper. "There was plenty of information before the match about which girls made the teams, and how the game was a big deal, and that everyone wanted to attend and volunteer to help out. But it's weird that after the game was over, it was as if the match never even existed in the first place."

"Look," I explained to him, "I've got so much going on right now. All of that stuff happened a long time ago, so I'm sure waiting a little longer to find out about it will be okay." Then I brushed him off, thinking that it probably didn't matter at all.

There was no time to worry about what happened seventy years ago. When I wasn't playing soccer, I planned my party because I was determined it would be the best time Darkmont had ever had. First, I used a computer program my dad had given me last year for my birthday and designed party e-vites to send to everyone. I cut and pasted a creepy haunted house, and used animation so that when you clicked on the door of the house, it opened to a bunch of dancing ghosts and skeletons. In spooky green letters that looked like melted wax, I wrote the date and time of the party. Everyone I e-mailed accepted.

Every time I logged on to MSN, I'd get a ton of instant messages – people asking if it was a costume party, wondering if I wanted them to bring any music. Being on the soccer team made me the most popular girl in town, and after the match it wouldn't matter what anyone thought because my friends and I would be having an amazing time at Grimoire School – as long as we won. Lately I simply assumed we would win and that life would only get better.

The rest of the week dragged by, and on Saturday afternoon, the day of the party, I was digging out a box in the attic where Mom had stored our old Halloween costumes. Inside the box was just what I was looking for: a black mask and a witch's hat. Those items, along with my soccer uniform of striped socks and black skort, would finish off the perfect costume.

Mia, Amarjeet, and even Emily from the Ghosts would be coming over soon to help me decorate. Mom had spent the whole week baking ghost- and witch-shaped cookies. Together we'd made caramel apple slices and pumpkin cupcakes. We went all out and made pizza bagels and filled bowls with tortilla chips. Throughout the entire afternoon, my head spun with excitement. When the sun started sinking, I hung out in the kitchen waiting for my friends to arrive.

Mom came downstairs and stood at the kitchen counter, hovering over a stack of file folders. For some reason, I got another one of my sinking feelings.

"Work called," Mom said. "I've got to get all the data from these files entered into the computer. And I have to do it tonight." She smiled, but I could see there were shadows under her eyes. Mom had been bringing work home almost every night, so she looked forward to the weekend break. "They're paying me double time. The money will be handy."

"But – " I stammered, my heart diving, "but you were going to keep Sookie up with you in the attic tonight, playing games and keeping her from pestering me at the party."

"Sorry," Mom said and shook her head. "There's no way I can keep her happy *and* get my work done at the same time. I'll still take my laptop up to the attic so that you don't have to worry about keeping the noise down, but you'll have to let your sister stay with you at the party."

This couldn't be happening. Mom had been so excited about my party. She'd helped me with all the plans. Making me watch Sookie would ruin everything. "But – " I repeated. There had to be some other solution.

"Sookie has to stay with you, or you can't have the party. Take it or leave it," said Mom.

At that moment, Mia and Emily showed up at the back door; I quickly nodded in agreement, but I burned with resentment. Nobody's little sister hung out with them at a party. Maybe she would be satisfied staying in the study watching movies. I could hope.

As far as costumes went, I quickly noticed that Mia and Emily had the same costume idea as me. Mia wore her Witches soccer uniform and had a spiked hat and tiny broom, and Emily wore her Ghosts uniform and had painted her face white with dark circles underneath her eyes. She actually looked really spooky. Before my friends even walked through the door, Sookie was hanging off of us, asking if she could play some of her little kid music, and didn't we think we should make popcorn balls, and don't we want to play "pin the broom on the witch" or a type of Halloween bingo she'd brought home from school?

"Oh, and Cat, you have to help me with my costume for tonight," Sookie said cheerfully. "I'm going to be a fairy princess."

So much for her keeping a low profile ... Emily rolled her eyes and Mia tried not to laugh. We all knew that Sookie was going to wreck this party.

"Here," Emily said. She handed Sookie the gloppy cobweb stuff. "Decorate the entrance hall with this. Make sure it hangs low so everybody gets that really icky feeling brushing through it when they first come in."

Clearly Emily had managed little sisters before, so I left Sookie up to her while I got up to my elbows in crepe paper, decorating the walls and ceiling. Soon my cheeks throbbed from blowing up dozens of orange and black balloons, and my nose burned from their rubbery smell. But then my mouth watered as we put the cookies and cupcakes out on a paper tablecloth decorated with a haunted house.

When I stood on a chair in the living room putting the finishing tack in all the streamers that gathered at the center of the ceiling, Emily handed up the finishing touch – a chandelier of balloons that she and Mia had wound together. Someone pounded on the back door, and I jumped down to answer it.

Jasper stood at the kitchen door. "Cat, you've been avoiding me again." He sounded irritated. "Whenever we agree to meet so that we can look into everything more, you don't show up. When I knock on your door, your mom says you're at practice. If I see you in the halls at school, you say you don't have time to talk about the first soccer match long ago."

Jasper pushed his glasses up on his head. "I found out who won the game, by the way. But I'm really worried."

"But the mystery is over," I said, smiling. "Just tell me, and then I can concentrate on the game and get back to my party."

"No, you don't understand," he said. "Remember I had rosters of both the Ghosts and Witches with all the girls' names? Up until the match, there was lots of information, but after the game, there was nothing." Jasper paced excitedly as if he was a detective cracking a big case. "So I thought, well, why not check the names of the girls on both teams and see who attended Darkmont the next year?"

Tapping my foot, I tried to be patient, but I heard a loud bang in the kitchen and wondered what Sookie was up to. "Cut to the chase," I said.

"The Witches must have won because after the match, not a single girl on that team returned to Darkmont." Jasper stopped dead and didn't look as satisfied as he should have for succeeding in his investigation.

When he didn't say anything, I sighed and asked, "Well, what's the problem?"

"Cat," he said. "I thought, why not cross-check the Witches' names with the Grimoire records just to make sure those girls got the scholarship?"

Only Jasper would think to dig through a bunch more files and double-check everything. Suddenly it occurred to me why he got straight As. "And?" I asked.

"Well," he said a bit apologetically, "I could only find one file from Grimoire in the library archives, and it only had student names up to the letter *h*. But every single girl on the Witches that should have been in that file wasn't. Those girls never ended up at Grimoire School either!"

"How many names did you actually match?" I was fidgety and wanted to get back to my party. Guests would be arriving soon.

"Only five names," said Jasper.

"Well that's it then, only five names. Those girls probably moved out of town or something." I looked over my shoulder. Sookie was messing around with the pizza platters and I hoped she wouldn't drop anything.

"Considering those were the only names I discovered, the odds would be slim that –"

"You do know," I interrupted, "that was ages ago, right?" What happened way back then meant less and less to me, and besides, I was in a hurry.

"Cat, we need your help in here!" shouted Mia.

Jasper leaned past me and checked out the balloons that Emily and Mia had finally hoisted up.

"Oh, by the way, I'm having a hard time getting my parents to agree to your Halloween party tonight." He looked a bit embarrassed. "My parents don't get Halloween."

"Huh?" In my defense, I was distracted at that moment, but his comment truly puzzled me.

"They don't celebrate Halloween." Jasper glanced longingly at the kitchen table decked with food. Sighing, he said, "Swarms of people in weird clothes climbing our stairs and banging on the door all evening freaks them out," Jasper shrugged his shoulders. "They might not want me to come, even though this is just a party about Halloween and not actually trick-or-treat night."

I'm sure my face looked blank. Suddenly his didn't.

"Oh. You don't really care if my parents let me come, do you? You never meant to invite me to your party in the first place." Jasper turned and raced down the back porch steps.

I was about to run after him – it wasn't that I hadn't planned on inviting Jasper. I hesitated on the porch. Try explaining to someone that you'd been so happy that all the popular kids wanted to come to your party that you'd forgotten all about him. That wouldn't exactly make him feel any better. So I didn't chase after Jasper.

"C'mon, Cat. People will be coming soon, and we still have to set up the playlists," called Emily.

Jasper had left, and there was nothing I could undo, so I consoled myself by thinking that he probably wouldn't have been allowed to come to the party anyway. I went back into the kitchen.

But as soon as the doorbell started ringing, I wished I'd tried to convince Jasper to come. For one thing, how was I going to entertain Sookie and still have a good time myself?

I couldn't shake the feeling that not inviting Jasper could be a big mistake.

CHAPTER 11

Day of the Dead

SOON THE HOUSE was full of vampires, witches, ghosts and zombies, cats and wizards. My heart flip-flopped when the boys' soccer team arrived, and I noticed that Zach was with them.

First I was running back and forth from the kitchen like a crazed windup toy serving snacks, until Mia and Amarjeet helped me carry platters to the dining room table. After that, Zach, who looked totally cute in his hockey jersey, and his friends helped fill the bathtub with ice and we threw all the soda in there. When I finally had a minute to catch my breath, I took the opportunity to set up my MP3 player. Then Mitch offered to be the deejay. Pretty soon, the music was going and everyone was dancing. I did a double take when I noticed Zach coming my way.

"Cat!" came Sookie's disgruntled voice, echoing out from the study. "I've been waiting and waiting. You haven't helped me with my costume yet!"

"Not now," I called cheerfully and kept smiling as Zach held out his hand, ready to get me out on the dance floor.

"Then get Mom!" Sookie shouted.

Zach rolled his eyes and said, "Your mom? Guess you'll be back soon."

"Oh, I promise," I said, waiting until I was in the hallway before muttering under my breath, "Yeah, sure, great idea – why not get Mom? Then I can have my mother *and* my little sister at my party." Banging open the door to the study, I asked huffily, "What do you want me to do?"

Sookie didn't sound a bit intimidated. "I need you to clip on my fairy wings."

A good fifteen minutes passed as I searched for enough safety pins to fasten the wings. Sookie had made her fairy costume out of old angel wings from a Christmas play. She explained that she painted brown spots all over the white feathers because fairy wings and angel wings were different. She also had some weird antennae contraption stuck to a headband and pulled over her ears. She wore Mom's sparkly purple top, which hung down to her knees and finished her costume off with her pink ballet slippers. She looked a bit ridiculous, and I felt embarrassed as she trounced out into the party and attracted smirking glimpses from the other guests.

Sookie put on *Ghostbusters* and insisted that everyone get up and dance to it. I hid in the kitchen, fetching more cookies and bagels. Then *Thriller* came on and I had to dance – I love that song. But it wasn't a couple's dance, and after that, every time I looked out on the floor, another girl was with Zach. It was all Sookie's fault!

As the evening wore on, more and more people came until the house was absolutely brimming. Almost everyone wore masks or lots of makeup, so I didn't recognize a bunch of people.

"Fairies don't really look like that," I heard a girl say to Sookie. The girl was dressed in black and she wore a beautiful silver mask.

"Then what *do* fairies look like?" Sookie demanded. After that, Sookie must have found an unsuspecting victim to play with because she'd stopped bugging me. Finally.

We ate and danced some more. Mitch, who'd painted himself green and had stuck a fish bowl on his head as a space helmet, started a conga line. We all joined and got really silly. We danced around the living room, out past the front porch, and out into the thick fog. We did the conga around two entire blocks and then we danced back to my house and collapsed in the kitchen laughing.

Although I could never quite maneuver my way back to Zach, the party was the most fun I'd ever had. Besides, I had a plan. For the last event of the night, we filled a big tub of water out on the back porch. Amarjeet and I dumped a huge bag of apples into the tub, standing back to avoid the splash. A dozen people lined up behind us ready to bob for apples. We were going to make two people dunk at the same time, a boy and a girl. Mia, Emily, and I had already planned who our partners would be. Just thinking about brushing my face up against Zach's gave me butterflies.

"Did you know that bobbing for apples – and other Halloween traditions – can be traced back to the ancient Celtic day of the dead?" came a voice out of nowhere.

Spinning around, I noticed a tall girl dressed in a long, black dress with high, black ankle boots standing behind me. She was the one who wore the silvery mask studded with shining white feathers. The mask looked kind of old-fashioned, like what people wore at masquerades in picture books. It also gave her an eerie, almost ghostly appearance. An odd smell surrounded her too – it was like a mixture of roses and cinnamon.

"What? What's Celtic?" I asked.

"Celts," the girl said, "were people who lived in Ireland and Scotland a couple of thousand years ago. The end of October was their festival of Samhain, the night when Celts believed creatures from the netherworld walked the earth."

The girl outlined the mask on her face, her fingers brushing the feathers. "Celts believed if you wore a mask, you could hide from the spirits of the netherworld – because this was a favorite disguise of the dead."

Creepy, I thought. Kind of like her. Who

exactly was she?

But I didn't have time to dwell on it because just then, Mitch and Mia bumped heads bobbing for apples, and Mitch accidentally fell up to his shoulders in the tub of water. Apples spilled out and everyone laughed as they bent over to start picking them up. I went into the kitchen to grab a mop and when I got back outside, the mysterious girl in the mask was gone.

That was it for bobbing apples, so I never did get a chance to brush up against Zach. The party ended shortly after that, and Emily and Mia stayed an extra hour to help me clean up. After they left, I was exhausted – it was that good, achy tired feeling that you get when you've had so much fun, you're about to drop. I climbed the stairs and walked past Mom's room. It was empty. She was still working up in the attic, but because I couldn't wait to jump into bed, I decided not to check in with her.

Even though I was tired to the bone, the party kept replaying in my head. Just as I began to get that drifty sleepy sensation, I remembered that I'd been kind of harsh to Jasper when he had stopped by. And after he left, I had been worried about making a mistake in not inviting him. But it all worked out, didn't it?

CHAPTER 12

A Dreadful Jolt

THE NEXT MORNING, I slept late, until weak light poked through my blinds. Rain pattered on my window, and the floor felt icy cold as I crawled out of bed, tiptoeing to my closet to find my slippers. Delicious smells drifted up from the kitchen, and I followed the scent.

Downstairs Mom had made pancakes. Realizing I was starved, I sat down and slathered the pancakes with syrup. While I ate, we talked about the party. I told her how much fun everyone had, and she told me how pleased she was that the house was tidy when she came down in the morning.

"I worked way past midnight," Mom said. "And I just can't understand – every time I got close to the bottom of my files, it was almost as if more files appeared on my desk." Mom sipped her tea and yawned. "I'm going to bed early tonight, that's for sure."

After I finished breakfast, I took our plates to the counter and began filling the sink with soapy water, but Mom shooed me away. "You should head up to the field early for practice," she said. "Remember, winning the scholarship is everything." Mom grabbed a dishcloth and wiped a plate.

Mom's major enthusiasm was still puzzling. But that was okay, because I didn't need any distractions.

Gathering up my soccer gear, I rushed off and met up with Mia and Amarjeet at the bottom of Grim Hill. They seemed almost as tired as Mom had been. By the time we'd hiked to the top of the hill, the rain started coming down hard, and Mia and Amarjeet looked like drowned rats. I guessed that I did too.

"Great party. I had an awesome time," Mia said, and then she yawned.

"Yeah, it was one of the best parties I've ever been to," said Amarjeet. Then she sneezed. "I'm getting a chill."

My feet were wet and squishy after hitting a few puddles, but once we got on the soccer field, the rain didn't matter. The castle school on top of the hill sang its song to me, and my body danced to the melody. Outrunning everyone, I could get the ball whenever I wanted and make it do whatever I wanted. My foot was the magnet and the ball acted as if it was made of steel – except when I aimed, kicked, and launched the ball past the other players and it landed exactly in the right spot.

After practice every muscle in my body ached. How long had it been since I'd skipped soccer even for one day? How long since I'd had enough time to finish my chores or do all my homework? Stopping in my tracks, I realized it had been quite some time.

For one thing, no teacher asked me to turn in my homework, which was helpful because I hadn't finished a single assignment. And during these last weeks before the match, every girl on the Ghosts and the Witches was dismissed an hour early from school for practice. None of the other students seemed jealous of our extra privileges. In fact, everyone was cheering us on.

I didn't mention how strange I thought everyone was behaving as I resumed trudging down the hill with Mia and Amarjeet. No point questioning a good thing. What was it people said? "Don't look a gift horse in the mouth?" What was the connection between that saying and the Greek myth about a gigantic hollow horse that soldiers had hid inside to sneak behind enemy lines, anyway? Those Greek guys should definitely have looked their gift horse in the mouth. Oh well, that's not what the expression advised. Saying goodbye to my friends, I turned down my street and wearily made my way home.

My legs felt stiff, so I went straight upstairs to the bathroom to pour a hot bath. I soaked in the tub until Mom called me down for dinner. We devoured homemade turkey vegetable soup and fresh baked biscuits.

No one had to tell me to go to bed early, and seconds after diving under my down comforter, I fell into a deep, exhausted sleep.

* * *

The next day, the thick fog that covered our town every night didn't clear until after school, when Mia, Amarjeet, and I climbed Grim Hill to the soccer field. Later, after another grueling but exhilarating practice, we said exhausted goodbyes at the bottom of the hill, and I went home.

When I went upstairs to my room to change my clothes, I passed by the bedroom door and noticed three long, white feathers on the wood floor. How had I missed them before? Picking one up, I stroked it. The feather felt silky and shimmered pink and green.

Sookie!

A terrible shock overtook me. Everything appeared to shrink and fade. I blinked my eyes, but it still seemed dark. Even though blood pounded in my skull, I took a deep breath and tried to think.

I hadn't seen or even thought about Sookie since halfway through my party Saturday night.

How could I have forgotten to tuck her in after the party or ask Mom where she was at breakfast or where she was during dinner last night? Had she made new friends? Was she invited to a sleepover? Of course that's what happened. Except there was one weird, upsetting detail. Until I picked up the feather, I'd completely forgotten the fact that I even had a little sister!

I threw open Sookie's bedroom door to check on her.

Her room was neat and tidy.

Terror clawed up my throat. Sookie's room was *never* neat and tidy. Forcing myself to take another deep breath, I figured Mom must have realized what a big mistake she'd made almost wrecking my party by ordering me to take care of Sookie. So she must have come downstairs during the party to get Sookie, then made her clean up her room. That sounded perfectly logical, so why was my heart racing and my stomach dive-bombing?

Inside the hamster cage, poor little Buddy stuck his pink nose through the bars and pawed at me with his tiny foot. His seed dish was empty. Thinking how unusual it was that Sookie forgot to feed him, I poured him some sunflower seeds. She loved Buddy and never forgot his food dish or water bottle, not ever. She acted like a mother hen when it came to her hamster.

Mom!

Mom hadn't mentioned Sookie at all yesterday. Not, "Oh, Sookie complained constantly about staying away from the party," not, "Oh, we had a good time together." Come to think of it, if Sookie *had* stayed upstairs, Mom would surely have said something.

I dropped the feather and watched it drift to the floor before I raced downstairs.

Mom was filling her briefcase with paper-work. She snapped up her case and grabbed her purse.

"You're back from soccer already?" Mom said, frowning slightly. "The coaches are cutting practice a little short, aren't they? By the way, Cat, I need to go back to Grimoire. They told me they want me to stay and work until later in the evening. There's an after-school event, and they want me to hold down the fort in the front office – I have to answer the phones and do the photocopying. Sorry, but you'll be on your own for dinner. The money will be great, so I can't pass it up."

Suddenly my throat dried up. Mom said "on your own." She didn't mention babysitting. She hadn't mentioned Sookie once. A cold dread crept up my spine. My fingers had felt hot when I stroked the feathers, and they still tingled – especially when I thought about how things were definitely wrong. How could I have forgotten all about my little sister?

"What's wrong?" Mom had picked up her bag again. She stared at me. "You look upset."

"Sookie." It came out in a whisper.

"Who?"

"Sookie, where is she?" This time I shouted.

"Calm down. Who is Sookie?" asked Mom.

Something even stranger started happening. My thoughts became jumbled, and I started forgetting why I was so upset. A second ago, I had been asking something important, but what was it? Now my fingers were oddly numb, and I rubbed them against my track pants while I stood there for a minute, studying the living room, wondering what was missing. A black and orange streamer hung down from the deflating balloon chandelier that I'd left up from my party. That night, the night of the party, someone had been standing under the chandelier, someone important. Closing my eyes, I tried to picture who it was, but all I could see was a girl with the white feathered mask. The feathers …

Slowly, almost as if I didn't want to know, I trudged back upstairs. I stared at the feathers on the floor for a second before I forced myself to pick them up. When I stroked them, they shimmered like a rainbow.

Then I remembered too much.

Sookie had disappeared. I hadn't watched out for her and halfway through my party, before the apple bobbing, she'd vanished. All I'd cared about that night was how she'd finally stopped bugging me. And now Mom didn't even remember her. And if I wasn't holding these feathers, I'd forget about little Sookie as well.

What was going on? Forcing myself to think, I recalled that Jasper had mentioned girls who had gone missing. If only I'd have invited him to the party. He'd have kept an eye on Sookie. Instead, it was as if she had been erased from our minds just like ... just like what?

When I shoved the feathers into my pocket, I got an idea. Rushing into my room, I grabbed a picture of Dad and Sookie. I took it to Mom. "Who is this?" I pointed to Dad's sunshine girl.

Mom studied the picture. She half-smiled – it was the kind of smile she used when she was careful to say the right thing. "Is it your dad's new stepdaughter?"

Dad didn't have a new family. As far as I knew, Mom hadn't even heard from him since we'd moved. She simply had no idea who Sookie was. Mom acting as if she never heard of Sookie was so unbelievable, it made me feel dizzy. But when I brushed the tips of my fingers against the tips of the feathers in my pocket, I knew things were very wrong. I had to hang on to that horrible feeling if I was going to find out what had happened to my sister. I kept the feathers in my pocket and wouldn't let Mom touch them. She would be so frightened if she remembered everything now. Letting Mom discover *I'd* lost Sookie wouldn't help.

It was up to me to find my sister.

CHAPTER 13

A Haunting Discovery

ONCE I PULLED myself together, I figured out three things. One – the girl in the mysterious mask had been trying to tell me something. Two – the feathers that had helped me remember Sookie were the same white feathers on that girl's mask.

Three – I needed Jasper.

Taking off at a run, I hurried next door, jumped the stairs three at a time, and pounded on Jasper's door. Jasper's dad, Mr. Chung, answered.

"Why hello, Cat. How's the soccer going? Are you ready for the big match?"

Not meaning to be rude, I blurted, "Is Jasper home?" At least I didn't shout in my panic.

Mr. Chung shook his head. "He's at the library."

On top of my pounding heart, I felt sick with guilt. Jasper had known something was wrong in this town. He hadn't given up investigating when all I'd cared about was my new popularity. Now I was in terrible trouble.

"Mr. Chung, have you seen Sookie?" I asked, hoping desperately he would remember my sister.

"Sookie ..." he said slowly. Mr. Chung squinted

past me up Grim Hill. For a second, I thought he knew who I was talking about, but he shook his head. "Who is this Sookie?"

My hope evaporated. I said, "Never mind," and was about to leave, but he gently grabbed my arm.

"Cat, you look so pale. Come in, I just made some fresh noodles."

The smell of garlic and ginger made my stomach grumble. Lunch was long past, but I muttered, "No thanks," turned, and ran down the stairs. Mr. Chung called after me as I headed toward the library.

"Something peculiar is in the air. You're going to need all your strength. You should come in and eat!"

Shivering, I kept running. A couple of blocks later, I spotted Emily and another girl from the Ghosts making their weary way home from soccer practice.

"Emily, did you notice when Sookie left the party the other night?" I gulped, catching my breath. Emily had given Sookie decorations to put up at the party. Maybe she'd –

"Who's Sookie?" they asked simultaneously.

Despite Mom and Mr. Chung forgetting about Sookie, I had expected Emily to laugh and say she had seen her – that she was just playing down the street or that she was still waiting for me up on the soccer field. Even though everyone seemed to have forgotten Sookie, I had a hard time believing any of this was real.

"Anyway, wicked party," said Kate, the other girl.

"Yeah, thanks for inviting your soccer rivals," Emily said smiling.

As they walked away, I touched the silky feathers in my pocket. If it wasn't for those feathers, it would seem as if everyone else was right and I was dreaming. A scary thought occurred to me. How did I know that this wasn't true? Would the feathers work on anyone else? I turned and kept running, even when I passed Zach and Mitch.

"Cool party Saturday night," Zach said. "Hey, I wanted to ask you something. Do you want to come to the dance with me next week?"

Who could think about dancing? I kept going.

"Don't forget to invite Mia!" Mitch called after me.

The town archives were in a small building built onto the library. Bursting through the door, I noticed right away that old has a smell. Those endless aisles of paper records smelled musty and dry – I could almost taste it. When I checked the first aisle, I found Jasper digging through a box on the bottom shelf. He gave me a cold look.

"How was your party?" he asked casually.

I burst into tears.

He walked over to me and fished for a tissue

from the pocket of his plaid shirt.

"It's okay," Jasper said. "I forgive you."

Actually I was crying about Sookie, but a few of those tears were for being a jerk and only caring about myself. Jasper was a good friend.

"Please tell me you have seen Sookie. She's missing," I blubbered.

"Sookie," he repeated a couple of times. "Sorry, Cat, but I don't know who you mean."

I slipped one of the large white feathers from my pocket and handed it to him.

The feather shimmered mauve and blue when Jasper touched it.

"What do you mean, Sookie's missing?" Jasper's eyes widened with alarm.

I told Jasper *everything* that had happened at my party and since my party, including his dad's and my mom's reactions.

"Mom can't even remember her own daughter," I finished. Sniffling, I blew my nose. "Besides the feather I gave you, I have two more. If I gave Mom one, it would only make her feel terrible. More than that, I think that if I want to find Sookie again, you have to keep that feather. And I'd better hang onto the third feather for a while longer, just in case."

Jasper looked thoughtful. "You'd better trust your instincts. At least while you're holding the feathers. No one else in this town is thinking clearly, and it's not just the forgetting. There's the obsession everyone has with the soccer match. If I hadn't been investigating what happened in the original game about seventy years back, I'd have gotten caught up in the excitement the same as everyone else."

Jasper had a point. Before, I jokingly thought that the anticipation of the soccer match had cast a spell over everyone in this town. Now it didn't seem funny at all. Not only did the feathers help me remember, but they woke me up to the fact that no one in this town had been acting normally since the tryouts. I mean, teachers saying "don't worry" about assignments? Right, that was *so* typical.

"We've got to find Sookie," I said, trying to hold back my tears.

"We can't panic," said Jasper, but the blood drained from his face as he paced back and forth. "Tell me again about that mysterious masked girl at the party. Wasn't she the last person you saw with Sookie? What was she saying to you?" Jasper clutched the other feather as he nervously rattled out questions.

"She was talking about Halloween traditions," I said. "She mentioned Celts, who I guess were these ancient people who had started a lot of Halloween customs we still practice, and she said –" I stopped. Remembering what she had told me while I was holding the feather was like seeing her stand right in front of me, all Halloweened-out in her old-fashioned black clothes, silver mask, and spider hairclip – the *ruby spider hairclip* – how had I missed that the first time? Finally, I recognized the tall girl.

"Jasper, the girl in the mask, I think it was Sookie's friend, that weird Goth girl, Cindy."

"Okay!" he shouted, pounding his fists together. The librarian peered over his desk at us. More quietly, Jasper confirmed, "Now we have a starting point. If Sookie's friend showed up at the party, the friend you didn't want her talking to –"

"Exactly," my heart sank as I thought about Sookie's stubborn streak. "And it would be just like Sookie to go somewhere else with Cindy, just so she could do what she wanted before I stopped her!"

For my sake, Jasper said very calmly, "We don't know that she left with Cindy, but we do know Cindy paid attention to her at your party, right?"

I winced because *I* hadn't paid attention.

Jasper shook his head saying, "This isn't your fault, Cat. Clearly there's something a lot stranger going on. Have you ever seen Cindy at Darkmont?"

Shaking my head, I said, "Definitely not."

"Then Cindy must be a Grimoire student. Here's the problem," Jasper waved at the endless aisles of boxes. "I've been looking up all the old school records here because Grimoire School has never put anything online, not even current stuff. I don't know how we'll learn Cindy's last name."

Puzzled, I said, "But Grimoire puts lots of stuff online; my Mom's always inputting and downloading student data files."

"It's locked, then," said Jasper. "No one from outside the school can access that information."

"What about daughters of school secretaries?" I said. "Mom's laptop is at home, and I'm sure I could figure out her password – she probably has it set to default." My mother could never remember passwords, so this was the first moment since Sookie disappeared that I'd felt hopeful. Jasper grabbed my hand and we flew out of the library, racing back to my house.

Since early this morning, I'd started running and hadn't stopped. My side ached and I was starting to feel light-headed, but I only paused a second to catch my breath before climbing up to the attic where Mom usually left her laptop. The way things were going, I half expected that to be missing, too. As we ducked under the low door, I felt relieved when I spotted the computer sitting on the desk.

When I turned it on, I was immediately logged in at Grimoire, but when I typed in Mom's name, we couldn't automatically access the records. "Now what?" I asked miserably.

"Type in her name and ask for a password hint," suggested Jasper.

The hint was "a six letter word for 'important.'" Mom always said the most important thing to her is "family," so I typed it in as quickly as I could. I logged on successfully and in seconds, I located the student registers at Grimoire School. Oddly, there wasn't a single Cindy at Grimoire, and there were no other schools in town. "We've hit a dead end," I said with deep disappointment. "Cindy must be homeschooled."

"This is crazy." Jasper paced the floor, sounding more and more alarmed. "Even if we call the police, they won't know what we're talking about. What if it's just like those other girls from the first match – the ones I can't find a single trace of after the first scholarship game?"

"Jasper," I said. Now it was my turn to take a steadying breath. "There's got to be some record of those first girls. I'm already in the Grimoire registry, so why don't you give me their names. I can easily go back in time with a click of the mouse." What I was really hoping for was *some* kind of connection.

"Here, I can do better than that." He handed me the entire list of Darkmont girls who'd registered for the first scholarship game.

"Remember," Jasper said. "I couldn't find a single name of any Witch team member registered at Darkmont after the soccer match. And I found only one old Grimoire file for all the registered names up to the letter *h*, so I know for sure that a few girls hadn't registered there, either."

Quickly I did a cross-check against all the names on Grimoire's register.

"Jasper, you were wrong," I said in a low, frightened voice. "After the scholarship match long ago, a *few* girls didn't go missing. None of those girls registered at Grimoire. The entire Witches team *vanished*!"

Both Jasper and I stood in stunned silence for a few seconds.

There had to be another explanation. Maybe a bunch of files simply went missing or were never entered in the first place. That's what I tried convincing myself. But in my heart, I thought that I might never see Sookie again.

"Jasper, we have to find Cindy – fast. The more I think about it, the more I know there was something not right about that girl. Why did she come to the party in the first place? And why did I only see her hanging out with Sookie? And there was all that weird stuff about Halloween she was telling me. She's our only clue." A dark feeling blossomed in my chest. "Jasper, I really think Cindy took my sister." Maybe not by force, but Sookie was gone all the same.

Jasper took off his glasses, rubbed his eyes, and put the glasses back on. He looked sick with worry, but I could tell he was trying hard to think of anything that would help.

When I pushed aside Mom's papers so Jasper could join me at the computer, some of her files slid off the desk and landed with a thud. Jasper bent over and picked them up.

"Eureka!"

Only Jasper would say "eureka." But I felt a gush of hope. "You found a file with Cindy's name on it?"

"No," said Jasper. "But I finally found Alice's old journal. It must have been mixed up in your mother's work stuff."

Why hadn't I thought of searching through the files before? Mom had been working a lot up in the attic, and her papers were always scattered all over the desk.

Jasper opened the journal. We turned back to the entries after Alice's sister, Lucinda, had left to play in the Halloween soccer match. We flipped through the pages.

November 1, I was picked to sing in the school concert, I read again. *Mother was pleased.*

Why hadn't Alice mentioned that her sister's team won the soccer match? The question still haunted me.

November 20, I got an invitation to Valerie Cromlin's birthday party.

December 25, Mother, Father, and I went to Grandma's for Christmas dinner. Faster and faster,

Jasper and I turned the pages.

February 14, I got twenty-six Valentines at the school party today. One valentine was trimmed in red lace and signed "anonymous." I hope it was from Jimmy Mason. Flip, flip, flip, we raced through the journal.

As I turned the pages again and again, a terrible dread made my head spin so badly, I had to stop reading and sit down on the old trunk. "Alice never wrote in her journal about who won the scholarship game," I said, but it was more than that. And now I knew what had bothered me so much about the journal.

"Right. It was as if ..." Jasper didn't finish. Instead, I did. "Alice never wrote about her sister again." My voice cracked as I said it.

Jasper turned to me, his brown eyes deeply troubled. "I was going to say, it was more like Alice never had a sister in the first place."

I began to shiver as if I'd just dunked my head into a tub of ice water.

What if Sookie wasn't the first girl to disappear *and* be forgotten? What happened to Alice's sister? Did she turn up later? Or were all the girls on her Witches team erased from everyone's memories? That just couldn't be.

Jasper said, "Look at this." He pointed to the back cover of the journal. *Alice Greystone.* "I didn't really pay attention to the name the first time we found this journal, but there's an old lady on my paper route, and I'm sure her name is Alice Greystone."

What were the chances this was the same Alice Greystone who owned the journal and who might have lost a sister a long time ago? Actually, for such a small town, pretty good. Besides, it didn't matter. It was the only lead we had.

"Where does she live?" I asked.

"27 Fairlane Street," said Jasper. "Not far from here."

Jasper tucked the journal under his arm, and we rushed out the door and down the leaf-littered streets.

CHAPTER 14

The Ghost Girl

FORTUNATELY, THIS LEAD had given me more energy, and I beat Jasper up to the wraparound porch of an old-fashioned house with stained-glass windows.

"Maybe we shouldn't get our hopes up," warned Jasper.

I didn't listen to him. Before he could say anything else, I hopped up the steps and banged three times on a brass knocker shaped like a lion's head. No one answered. Just as my heart started to sink, the door opened, and an old woman in a brown tweed suit stood in front of us.

"Why hello, dear," the old lady said, smiling past me and at Jasper. "Have you come to collect for the paper?"

"No, um, Mrs. Greystone, may we come in?" asked Jasper.

"It's 'Miss,' dear. I've just made a pot of tea. Why don't you join me?" Miss Greystone waved us through the door.

Her house had dark wood paneling that matched the floors. Rose- and leaf-patterned rugs were scattered under old-fashioned furniture. Lace doilies covered every chair and table, and the warm rooms smelled of lemon wax and tea.

Miss Greystone bustled in the kitchen while Jasper and I fidgeted on the red velvet couch. Before she could even pour the steaming tea into our cups, I blurted out, "Do you have a sister?"

Miss Greystone laughed. "Why no, dear, I am an only child." At that, Miss Greystone lost her smile. The skin around her eyes crinkled and she seemed a bit sad all of a sudden.

I couldn't hide my disappointment because I had to find out what happened to the girl in the journal – it was all too similar to what happened to Sookie. But the journal could have belonged to some other Alice Greystone.

Jasper pulled out the journal, which he had tucked in his jacket. Holding it out, he asked, "Did this ever belong to you?"

Miss Greystone's eyes lit up. She eagerly reached for the journal. "Wherever did you get this?" Miss Greystone gently flipped the pages. "My goodness," she said laughing.

"In my attic," I said and then told her where I lived.

"My family lived in that house until we moved here," Miss Greystone said wistfully. "I had happy times there."

"But you wrote about a sister," Jasper said politely and pointed to several journal entries.

For a few seconds, Miss Greystone was quiet. Then she sighed and patted the journal affectionately. "Back then I considered myself a budding writer," she said. "I wanted to publish stories, and I made up fanciful tales to make my life all the more interesting." Her smile slipped. "I used to imagine what it would be like to have an older sister. Being an only child is a lonely thing."

Jasper nodded in agreement.

I got that feeling again – like when the picture on the T.V. fades out and the room gets darker. It made perfect sense that she would have made up her sister. It sounded exactly like something Sookie would have done if she'd been an only child. As it was, Mom, Dad, and I had to put up with an imaginary brother until she was five. I clutched the two feathers in my pocket. *Sookie, Sookie, Sookie*, I whispered to myself. It didn't matter if we were wrong about the journal. Things didn't add up, and my sister was still missing.

"Thanks for the tea," I said even though I hadn't taken a sip. "We've got to go."

Jasper offered to help Miss Greystone carry the tray back to the kitchen.

"Don't worry about the tea tray, just go ahead. It looks as if you have important things to do," Miss Greystone said kindly.

As I stood up, I noticed a black-and-white photograph on the mantel. I went over and peered closely at the faded picture of two girls. It was a close-up photo of their faces. The first girl was quite young and wore her straight, blond hair short, the same as Sookie. The first thing I noticed about the older girl was that she wore an unusual barrette in her hair. *A ruby spider weaving its silver web!* The older girl in the picture looked like the same Goth girl who had hung out with Sookie on the soccer bleachers during my soccer practices, who had worn the strange mask at my party, who had spoken to me about ancient Celts – and who most likely had taken my sister somewhere!

The other girl *was* Cindy. My adrenaline surged.

Grabbing the picture in my hand, I almost shouted, "Is this a relative or friend of yours?"

Miss Greystone studied the photograph. First she pointed to the little girl with blond hair. "That's me when I was eight." Miss Greystone then pointed to Cindy. "For some reason I have always loved this picture, even though I've long forgotten who that other girl was."

Cindy was in a picture taken over seventy years ago. How could that be? How could the girl I'd spoken to at my party be over eighty years old? The room spun. Basically, I faced an impossible situation ... unless I'd been talking to a ghost – no, there had to be another explanation.

Then I got an idea. I pulled out the third feather from my pocket and handed it to Miss Greystone.

"It's lovely, dear." She stroked its silky tip.

The feather shimmered silver and gold, but it didn't stop there. The feather began to glow, and I worried that it might burst into flames.

Miss Greystone stared at the photograph I held in my hand. After a few moments, a tear trailed down her cheek.

"Please, dears," she almost whispered. "Sit down again and tell me why you've come here."

* * *

Our tea grew cold as I finished telling Miss Greystone what Cindy had told me about Halloween traditions the other night at my party and how my little sister had disappeared.

Miss Greystone kept clutching the feather, stroking it as she stared at the old photograph. "When I hold onto this feather, I remember now, all those years ago," said Miss Greystone. She dabbed her eyes with a hanky. "Lucinda was my sister; everyone called her Cindy. She was in a big soccer match at Grimoire School. Her team won and – and after that, I don't remember anything about what happened to her. I *know* she existed, but it seems as if it were all a dream."

As she handed me back the feather, I shook my head and didn't take it. "Hold on to it, or else you'll start to forget again." Even with the feather, it took everything in my heart to believe Sookie was real.

"Over seventy years," Miss Greystone said thoughtfully. "If you really think you talked with my sister, she couldn't be young. She'd be older than me."

Impossible or not, I knew I'd been talking to Miss Greystone's sister the other night, and she was my age. "All I know is that the last time I saw Sookie," I said, "she was talking to your sister. That can't be a coincidence, considering Cindy – I mean – Lucinda's been missing all these years, and then my sister goes missing." Again I was close to tears.

Jasper shoved his glasses up on his head. "Lucinda's disappearance and reappearance has got to do with Grimoire School and the soccer game. She vanished seventy years ago after the school's first scholarship game. Cat, your match is on Sunday. Lucinda showed up at your pre-game party. There's definitely a reason."

With all that was going on this morning, I had forgotten the game was this coming weekend. Shivers crept up my spine. I swallowed and said, "There's something else. I know Sookie is with Lucinda, because I feel it in my heart. She came and got Sookie and took her away. But why? She was trying to tell me all that stuff about Samhain, so it's got to be important."

"We need more information," said Jasper. "We

should leave and split up. I'll go up to Grimoire myself and see if I can slip into the office and find out anything about the original soccer match." He looked at me. "Cat, you could search for Celts and Samhain online."

"I'll do a search, too," offered Miss Greystone.

They had a good plan, except for one thing.

"You should be the one to go online," I told Jasper. "It makes more sense for me to search Grimoire School." He shook his head no. Before he could say anything, I reasoned, "Mom's working tonight, and all I have to do is pretend I'm visiting her at the school, and then I can sneak around and try to investigate."

He couldn't argue with that. They both agreed I had a point, but Miss Greystone appeared extremely nervous when she said, "Cat, you be very careful up at that place. I've lived in this town all my life – Grim Hill and that school have never seemed safe to me."

That's exactly the way Sookie felt. She always said how much she hated that school on the hill. If only I'd listened to her.

I had to hurry and find her. As I left Miss Greystone's house, Jasper called out to me, "By the way, you do know what the word 'grimoire' means, don't you?"

I had no idea, so I shook my head.

"It's a word I've read in horror stories, and it

means 'a witch's magic spell book.' It's what witches use to conjure spirits and demons. So be careful." Jasper sounded worried.

"It's just a name," I said, but I swallowed and a hard lump sat in my stomach as I kept going in the direction of Grim Hill.

CHAPTER 15

A Wicked Revelation

I **CLIMBED UP** Grim Hill, past the blazing woods of crimson and yellow leaves, up to the school at the top. The sun was hanging low, and it was almost early evening. At least the fog had lifted. Mom had told me she'd be working past dinnertime, so it made sense that I would pretend to visit my mom and then search the school. Simple. Then why was I completely terrified?

Forcing my legs forward, I approached Grimoire School. Despite its dark mystery, I couldn't help but think that the building itself was beautiful. It was as if some giant had dropped a fairy castle on top of the hill. Red ivy hung from the school's walls and brick turrets. Clusters of oak and hawthorn trees surrounded the school and thickened to woods that crept down the hill to my street.

But something made me slow down and stop in front of the wide wood doors of the school. The iron handle felt icy cold as I tugged it open and stared into the dim, cavernous entrance hall. I stepped into the shadows.

The empty halls of black-and-white checkered floors stretched out endlessly, and I walked along until I noticed a sign that said "administration" pointing up one stairway. On the first landing, I found my mom's cubbyhole of an office. Mom was hunched over a desk stacked up so high with files, you could barely see her. As far as I could tell, she was the only person in the whole place.

"Hi, Mom," I said finally. She hadn't even noticed me standing there.

Mom peeked over her files and smiled, but she looked distracted. "Cat, what are you doing here?"

Up until that second, I hadn't thought about an excuse, but I said, "Um, I went to the library and forgot my key. I'm locked out of the house."

Mom sighed and said, "Well, at least you remembered your head," like she always said when I forgot stuff. Part of me wanted to break down over how normal her reaction was. It made me realize just how strange things had become. But I bit my lip until I felt more in control, and then I smiled back at her.

She grabbed her purse and dug out her key. "You're lucky I always carry a spare."

Saying "Thanks," I pocketed the key, but instead of leaving out the main doors, I started exploring the halls on the second floor. There had to be another office, a bigger one that had more information about the first Halloween soccer match.

I kept walking along the tiled floor. The stained glass near the ceiling let in blood-colored light, which gave the place a spooky atmosphere. And although the school appeared deserted, with the exception of my mother, I thought I heard the echo of footsteps behind me or hushed voices in a classroom. But when I opened the heavy arched oak doors and peeked inside, I saw nothing.

Hanging in the hall was a series of portraits of teachers and former students. I studied their faces. They all showed a strong resemblance to one another – it was as if they were from the same family.

But there was something else.

The Grimoire girl who had been the goalie at the soccer tryouts looked just like the people in the portraits. Then I realized that she and the other students in the paintings were slightly smaller versions of our soccer coaches. The coaches, the girls, and the teachers in the portraits all had pointy chins, odd eyes that seemed almost too large for their faces, thin noses, and long, straight hair. They weren't identical, but they were eerily similar to one another. At practice, I'd never really paid attention to the coaches or the occasional Grimoire girl, but seeing all these same faces lined up together on the wall, you couldn't miss the resemblance.

Following the portraits to the end of the hall, I spotted the library. At least that's what the sign above the door said. When I stepped inside and closed the door behind me, I saw that the room was tiny and ancient. The scene could have been a picture from an old-fashioned book. There were tall, skinny shelves and long, narrow windows to the floor. And while it had the same papery smell of a library, there was only one book – a gigantic, fat book that lay open on a pedestal and was surrounded by the same wispy fog that crept down the hill to cover the town at night. When I took a closer look, though, the fog was streaming *from the book* and drifting out a nearby open window. I kept telling myself that this couldn't really be happening. Then the pages began to flip by themselves! I jumped back.

When the pages stopped turning, a white feather bookmark, identical to the one in my pocket, marked an open page. My heart pounded in my ears as I edged closer to the book. *What did Jasper say 'grimoire' meant? A magic book?* I was now convinced that's exactly what I'd discovered.

The page had opened to a section titled "Lesson 439: Protection of Fairy Hills for Creatures of the Netherworld." There was a large illustration. Suddenly I didn't care that the book had been turning the pages all by itself, and I bent down to take a look.

Strange creatures filled the page – some of them resembling those figures in puzzle books that are divided in three sections, and when you flip the pages, the bodies, legs, and heads never match up. Shivers ran up my back. Other creatures looked a lot like, well, the students and teachers of Grimoire. They had the same pointy chins, long noses, and straight hair – like the coaches and the portraits in the hall. The passage underneath said:

Fairies and creatures of the netherworld: You must always use your glamour to avoid being discovered by humans. Only the most powerful spells will trick humans into believing that their haunts have not been invaded by fairies. Deceive their ears, trick their eyes, and make them think that carrying out your commands are their own desires.

But creatures of Grim Hill beware: Young children can be resistant to glamour. At times, they can see through the spell and recognize creatures from the netherworld. Most often, their adults will consider this as a child's imagination, but in some cases, you must employ other enchantments to remain safe. Most importantly, NEVER let any human possess any item from Fairy, because that human cannot then be enchanted.

The white feather from my pocket was exactly the same as the feather bookmark in the enchanted grimoire book. A fairy possession helps keep away the glamour. I *knew* my feather had powers! Was it helping me resist a fairy spell?

Suddenly there were voices in the hallway. I hid behind the door and peeked out of the skull-shaped keyhole. A troop of girls straggled behind Ms. Maliss, the coach with the long, white hair.

I had to do a double take, because I could see right through all of them!

"Now girls, keep an orderly formation," the coach said.

"It's hard when we're like this," complained one girl. As she spoke, her feet drifted up off the ground. She floated toward the ceiling until another girl grabbed her foot.

Choking back a gasp, I practically poked my eye right through the keyhole as I spied on them. I held my breath so I could hear them better and more importantly, so they couldn't hear me.

Ms. Maliss stopped in front of the classroom right across the hall from me. She looked up at the girl who was bobbing in the air like a balloon on a string.

"Now Ariel, you are a second-year student, and you should be able to manage your glamour better," Ms. Maliss said.

Ariel gave a sigh of dismay. "I'm trying ... but lots of us second years are losing our control."

"Don't worry too much," Ms. Maliss said and barked a cruel laugh – "the Halloween match is less than a week away. Once the event is over, and the winning team is awarded their scholarship," at this point she chuckled, "we'll all be as solid as this door for another seventy years." Ms. Maliss tried opening the door, but her fingers kept slipping through the doorknob.

"Oh well," she said. "I'd better save my energy for the soccer practices and the big game." The coach and the girls drifted down the hall to a classroom where the door was already open.

My throat felt like sandpaper when I swallowed. After a few terrified moments, I crept carefully back to the book. As my heart beat like a drum, I took my own white feather, held it in my shaking hand and said quietly, "I need to find out more about the students and teachers of Grimoire School."

Sure enough, the grimoire's pages flipped forward. When they stopped, the open page in front of me was titled "Lesson 667: Tithes and Fairy Circles." The illustration on that page revealed a large bonfire and a circle of what must have been strange creatures of the netherworld and human children dancing around the fire. I began to read:

Creatures of Grim Hill: Every seventy years you must exact a tithe. Capture human slaves and you will keep the link from your world and their world open.

On Samhain night, when the boundary veil between our world and the human world is thinnest, roam the hill and capture young sacrifices. Bring them to the fairy circle to dance with the fairies for the rest of their lives. The energy from this celebration will maintain the fairy link for another seventy years.

An urgent thought hit me – I knew exactly which human sacrifices Ms. Maliss and her students were waiting for.

I had to get away. *Now.*

Slipping out of the library, I ran down the hall as if the demons of hell were after me. If those ghostly girls were fairies, I didn't think they were the kind of fairies who brought kids money when they lost a tooth – not even close.

But I slid to a halt just before I flew down the stairs and burst out of the main doors. My mom sat in the little cubbyhole and worked away at her desk. She looked like a robot or worse, like some slave under a spell.

"Mom," I urged. "Come home with me. Don't stay here."

She looked up from her work. At first she seemed distracted again, and then she tilted her head as if she heard something.

"Cat, you should leave. You don't want my boss to see you here."

It wasn't what she said. It was the way she said it. She didn't have to tell me twice.

As I ran out of the school and onto the field, tears stung my eyes. How could I ever have wanted to be a student at this school? I stumbled past the old picnic area that Sookie had been afraid of.

Something stopped me in my tracks.

In the darkening shadows, a girl with black hair, black old-fashioned clothes, and black eyes, stood in the middle of the thickets and brambles.

It was Lucinda.

CHAPTER 16
The Despicable Truth

"**YOU KNOW WHERE** Sookie is!" I cried.

"She was in danger and I tried to rescue her." Lucinda sounded faint, as if she was much farther away from me.

"What do you mean *tried*?" I said in alarm.

"The coaches have terrible powers." Lucinda's voice grew even weaker. "Maliss and Sinster knew Sookie could see through the glamour to what was inside Grim Hill. And she was realizing the truth about the soccer match."

"So give her back to me and let her tell me herself," I insisted.

"I can't," Lucinda said mournfully. "Your sister was like a pesky fly that they were going to swat. I tried to help but –"

"But what?" I asked dreading the answer.

"I made a deal with the coaches." Lucinda wavered back and forth as if she was a flimsy paper doll. "I bargained that I would stop trying to warn you about the match if they let me protect your sister."

"So you just waltzed into my party and took Sookie?" I was trying to understand.

"The coaches tricked me," Lucinda said in anger. "I brought her to the fairy circle, and now – "

"Just tell me!" I demanded.

Lucinda began to fade like a watermark drying in the sand. "The problem is when I try to tell you anything directly – "

And then Lucinda vanished.

I began running down the hill. At the bottom, I turned and looked at Grimoire School as the sun sank completely behind it and the sky grew dark. The fog that had flowed out of the grimoire book of enchantment began creeping down the hill as if it was following me. There was no way I'd go back to that school again.

I sprinted past my house and back to Miss Greystone's. Before knocking, I wiped my face with my sleeve, trying to keep it together for Sookie's sake. When I knocked and Miss Greystone opened the door, she took one look at me and ushered me inside.

Miss Greystone brought me a tissue and I blew my nose. Forcing myself not to sound hysterical, I told her about how Lucinda took Sookie so she could protect her from the coaches, who were evil fairies, and that Lucinda should have –

"Slow down, Cat. Take a sip of water." Miss Greystone handed me a glass, saying, "I don't think I heard that last bit correctly."

After downing the entire glass, I told her the

rest – about Grimoire's transparent students and about what I'd read in the grimoire book about fairy hills and circles.

"The book was magical," I exclaimed. "But not in a happy, fun sense. There was a darkness about it." I shuddered. "But I don't get it," I said. "If those students aren't human, they aren't like any fairies I've ever read about. They weren't tiny creatures with wings. They seemed dangerous."

"My dear," said Miss Greystone, "real fairies *are* dangerous. My mother was from Ireland and told me many fairy stories – and not the cute little tales one sees in movies and storybooks today. In the past, everyone feared fairies. When people called them the good folk, they did that because they didn't want fairies to hear them say anything bad about them."

I blew my nose again. "But just what is the connection between fairies and Halloween?"

"Halloween has *everything* to do with those creatures of the netherworld," said Jasper who had slipped in quietly.

Jasper seemed too upset to sit still and explain. Instead he paced the room and pulled at his glasses. That used to annoy me. But now I hoped it meant he was onto something.

"I read that fairies are enchanters with supernatural powers who live in the netherworld, a kind of different dimension, which can be tucked inside a hollow hill," Jasper explained.

I nodded. The grimoire was filled with information about the netherworld.

Jasper went on, "In ancient Celtic times, a couple of thousand years ago, the Celts were onto fairies. The Celts knew how to protect themselves and take precautions. For one thing, when the veil got thin on Halloween night, called Samhain, the Celts threw a festival where they all stayed together. That festival must have been big because while most of us don't know it, we still celebrate a lot of the same traditions."

"That's what Lucinda said," I explained. "And she said the traditions were important." Whenever I mentioned Lucinda's name, Miss Greystone got such a sad look.

Jasper leaned forward with his face pinched so tight, I could tell he was extremely worried. "On Samhain night, the fairies will roam around to capture human slaves. That's where our custom of wearing masks came from. People would hide behind masks to confuse fairies into thinking they weren't humans, that they were also creatures of the netherworld."

I told Jasper and Miss Greystone what I'd overheard the soccer coach say, about how they'd soon be capturing new slaves so they could all be strong for another seventy years.

Miss Greystone gasped. "First they kidnapped

my sister and her friends. Now seventy years have passed and they need a new tithe. So they've captured your little sister, and they're looking for more sacrifices," Miss Greystone dabbed her eyes with a handkerchief.

"So," I added, "they can keep the bridge open between both worlds, which makes Grimoire teachers and students strong." The whole time I was talking, I stared at the old photograph on the mantel and was sickened by the thought of Lucinda dancing year after year. I wondered if that was now Sookie's horrifying fate.

Following my gaze, Miss Greystone whispered with disgust, "And the fairies keep the slaves until their human lives are almost over. When they've used them up, the fairies capture more young people."

"The soccer match is how they pick us." I held back my rage. "As soon as I overheard Ms. Maliss, I figured out that the soccer field is where they select the best slaves – by choosing the winning team." And none of us, not Emily on the Ghosts team, not Mia or the other Witches, realized we were like plump turkeys being eyed by a farmer right before Thanksgiving.

"But why hasn't Lucinda changed at all?" I asked. "She looks to be my age right now, the age when she was captured seventy years ago. How can that be?"

"Time passes differently in Fairy. If people manage to escape," and then Jasper spoke in a gentler tone, "I mean, *when* Lucinda and Sookie come back, Lucinda will probably age quickly. So we'd better get Sookie back soon, while she's still a little girl."

We all sat in silence. A cloud of doom settled over me as I mumbled, "What if there is no coming back?"

"Wait, Cat," Miss Greystone said and then walked over to the photograph of Lucinda and picked it up. "I'm wondering how my sister has managed to escape from Fairy, if only for short periods of time."

The cloud of doom slowed its descent – that was a good point. "Something about Sookie must have drawn Lucinda out," I said. "We need more answers." I stabbed my feather as if it was a sword. "We have to find out more about fairy circles. We have to help Sookie and Lucinda escape for good."

Miss Greystone reached over to her bookshelf. She brought down a very old volume and blew the dust off the cover. The title was *Celtic Myth and Fairy Tales*.

"This was my mother's book. I'll start skimming through it right away, in case it offers any clues," she said.

"But we still need a lot of other information

about Celts and tithes, and we need it fast," said Jasper. "If you've got the book, maybe Cat and I can go online."

"Two of us searching separately will be faster," I said. "Using my computer at home will speed things up."

"Then we'll reconvene in a couple of hours," said Miss Greystone.

After I left Miss Greystone's and walked to my house, I didn't go in right away. Instead, I sat down on the curb on top of a pile of leaves. The tang of the leaves' musty smell filled my nose. I bent over and put my head between my legs and let the blood rush to my brain. When would I wake up from this horrible dream? This wasn't happening. It couldn't be. When my eyes began to ache, I sat back up. Then I pinched myself – twice. It hurt.

Unlike Miss Greystone, I wasn't brought up on Celtic myth and fairy lore. Nor was I a bookworm like Jasper who always allowed his imagination to run wild. They say "Seeing is believing." But despite what I'd seen, it was really hard for me to believe any of this. A better explanation would be that I had gone crazy or was in some grisly coma, stuck in a permanent nightmare. I looked at my house, it was unlit and empty. Mom was never home, and Sookie had disappeared. This was my reality.

Sighing deeply, I stood up and brushed off the damp leaves that had stuck to my pants. There was only one thing to do.

First I went into my dark house and turned on the hall light. I rummaged in the closet and took out the black Halloween mask that I had worn at my party.

Then I began to trudge back up Grim Hill in the fog. Every step I took made my heart pound harder, but there was one book that held more information on fairies than anything I could find on the internet. *Always check a direct source*, my teachers often said.

One more peek at the enchanted grimoire wouldn't hurt – would it?

CHAPTER 17

Dancing to Death

IT WAS BAD enough crunching over leaves up Grim Hill in the dark with only a thin thread of light bobbing from my flashlight, not to mention that I was slipping on slimy things I didn't even *want* to see. But when the school loomed ahead in the shadows, I wondered how I ever thought Grimoire was beautiful. At night, the building lost its inviting appeal. Under the moon, it appeared haunted.

After forcing myself toward the front door, I tugged on the frozen handle. Part of me, a very large part, hoped the door would be locked, but it wasn't. I slipped inside.

Before I walked up the stairs, I put on the Halloween mask, hoping those ancient Celts were right about a disguise confusing the spirits of the netherworld.

The school sounded a lot more populated in the evening. Voices rang out of every classroom. Shadows of barely visible girls gathered at the end of the hall, so I hid behind the staircase until several of them passed by. Once they were gone, I came out of hiding, determined to make my way back to the library.

"You're missing the riddling session," said a voice near me.

I turned in surprise. A girl wearing the Grimoire uniform – a black silk tunic with purple and orange pinstripes – had crept up from behind. The girl wasn't completely solid looking, but she was less transparent than the students who had followed Ms. Maliss around when I was here earlier.

"You'll be late." She stared at me unfazed by my mask, as if it was completely normal.

Struggling to find my voice, I said, "Um ... I just forgot something," and glanced vainly down the hall.

What a relief when the ghostly girl only shrugged her shoulders and scurried away. Okay, score one for the Celts. They knew what they were talking about with the masks. I headed for the library, hugging the shadows of the hall, not particularly wanting to meet up with anyone else.

Once I got to the library, I allowed myself a tiny sigh of relief as I crept inside and shut the door. The grimoire sat open and fog was no longer drifting out from its pages. Instead, the fog was *pouring* out. Part of me wondered if I slammed the book shut, could I stop the enchantment of the town? Then I remembered the main reason I was here and that I couldn't risk anything until I found Sookie.

The grimoire was still open to the section on

fairy circles. Slipping my mask up so I could see better, I pulled my feather out of my pocket, trying to decide exactly what I had to know about fairies in order to get Sookie and Lucinda back.

Suddenly, the handle of the library door clicked.

Someone was coming in.

Desperately, I searched the tiny room for a place to hide. The empty bookshelves stood right against the wall; there wasn't even a desk to crouch behind. After another click and a soft hiss, the door cracked open. In a flash I ducked behind the thick green velvet curtain that hung from the narrow library window.

From behind the curtain, I could hear the muffled patter of footsteps across the marble-tiled floor. Dust clogged my nose and scratched my throat. My eyes watered, but I didn't breathe, let alone flinch, terrified of causing a ripple in the heavy cloth.

First a tap, then a rolling thud and a loud crash echoed through the room as the floor shuddered and the curtain shook. I gave the curtain the slightest tug and peeked around it.

An entire bookcase had opened up like a door, revealing a dark passageway with stairs spiraling down. The Grimoire girl I'd just seen ducked inside and disappeared into the darkness. A few moments passed, and the bookshelf began to rotate back toward the open wall, gears groaning and wood creaking. Without hesitation, I leaped from behind the curtain and ran toward the shrinking doorway.

But then I wasn't sure what to do. Here was a secret passageway inside the school – what was Grimoire hiding? Did I have the courage to follow the girl? Not even close. But I wanted answers, so before I could change my mind, I shoved my body between the closing bookcase and jammed my flashlight between the shelf and the wall to keep the hidden doorway slightly open – not enough to draw attention to anyone passing by the room, I hoped, but enough to keep the door from slamming shut. Once I stood on the top step, I noticed it was a good thing the passage door was ajar. Otherwise I'd be surrounded by complete darkness. No, it wasn't exactly pitch-black, for down the endless staircase far below, I could see the tiniest prick of orange light. There wasn't enough light to tell how far the Grimoire girl had gone, so I made myself count to one hundred twice before beginning my descent.

Inside the passageway, it smelled both musty and spicy, like moldy incense. The narrow stone steps were worn smooth – in other words, treacherous. For extra balance I kept one hand against the rough rock wall, but on about my hundredth step, something furry brushed by my hand – if it was a spider, it was gigantic. After that, I continued down with my arms close to my sides.

A cold draft cut through my clothes and sank into my bones. My eyes began to ache from the chill, but I kept going. When I was about one-third of the way down, what started as a *whoosh* built up to a deafening roar. Suddenly the air moved all around me and high-pitched squeals grated my ears. My heart leaped – bats! I hunkered down as low as I could on the steps, grateful my mask was perched on my head, covering my hair. The bats flew so close, my clothes twitched from their vibration and I caught their feral scent. After they passed, it took a moment before my legs stopped shaking and I could climb steadily down the stairs. The orange light grew slowly to the size of a soccer ball and then a giant beach ball, until it was clear that the passageway was leading me far beneath Grimoire School and into Grim Hill. When I stood at the mouth of the passageway, I realized why the light was orange. Being outside didn't put me back into any familiar surroundings. For one thing, the *whole sky* outside happened to be orange – as if someone had smeared the sky with pumpkin.

A quick look revealed another startling discovery – it seemed as if I was standing *on* the soccer field outside of Grimoire School, *yet I wasn't*. The soccer bleachers and goal posts were transparent, as if one image was superimposed over the other, so I was standing in two worlds at once. The flames of a bonfire roared and crackled in the middle of the field. Slipping my mask back over my face, I moved closer.

And then I heard it.

Music eerily similar to what I'd heard when I played soccer was now affecting me in a different way. Instead of buoying me on the field so I could play the best soccer of my life, this music made my feet twitch and my legs jump, and I could barely resist the urge to dance.

The others that swarmed around the bonfire couldn't resist the music either. The Grimoire girl I'd followed out of the library had joined a circle of dancers. She was kicking up her heels, her long black hair flying out behind her. As she spun, she turned and grinned at me, baring all her teeth in a razor-sharp smile. A slim boy with long arms and legs that sprang like coils in Slinky toys, bounced manically around the fire. He turned his head in a complete circle and I saw that his face was covered with the mask of a stork-like creature with a long, skinny beak. When he laughed, it was as if needles stabbed my skin. Half-human and half-goat creatures clip-clopped like tap dancers. Their eyes were fiery red and horns poked out of their hair. Girls with pure white hair and skin, dressed in long white cobweb gowns, glided around the fire.

I'd found the fairy circle.

And I could have easily been observing witches, devils, monsters, and ghosts dance around the fire. I finally understood how Halloween characters had spun from Celtic legends and fairy lore.

Amongst these creatures danced eleven girls dressed in old-fashioned clothes like Lucinda's. Now I could see that the clothes were soccer uniforms girls wore long ago. I could also see that unlike the fairy creatures, the girls weren't enjoying the dance.

I stared at the Witches team from the first match and watched them dance around the fire. None of the girls appeared any older than me, but each looked as if she'd been dancing for a long time. As one girl twirled past me, she moaned and tried to pull off one of her leather boots. Thin streaks of blood had climbed up her socks past her ankles. Another girl stumbled and fell to her knees until the boy with the stork mask poked her with his beak until she got up again.

One girl twisted and twirled, jumped and somersaulted, crying out, "I'm tired – please, I want to stop!"

"Go ahead," said the black-haired fairy girl with a cruel smile.

The girl stopped for a second, but then her legs began to twitch. Her feet began shuffling, and her body lurched forward. Soon she was dancing as hard as before.

My own legs trembled more and more. My body swayed to the manic music. Then Lucinda twirled past me.

"Get out fast," she urged. "It's all up to you. If you can't stop this, eleven more girls will take our places." She had no trouble seeing through my disguise.

"*Where is Sookie?*" I demanded. "I'm taking her with me!"

And as I spoke, I realized I hadn't been completely right about the dance. I spotted one girl who had not grown tired of the fairy circle. In fact, she giggled and laughed, twirling with stork boys and ghost girls.

"Sookie!" I called out.

Sookie looked up and didn't even seem to care that I was there.

I called to her again. She ignored me and ran to the other side of the circle and dodged between the two fairy girls in white.

"What's happened to her?" I began to chase after her. Before I could take a second step, Lucinda grabbed my arm and held me back. She swayed from side to side unable to keep still.

"Maliss and Sinster bargained with me," Lucinda explained. "They promised they wouldn't harm Sookie if I fetched her and had her spend a few moments of fairy time in the circle – so that she would stay out of their way until the match was over. That way, neither she nor I could directly tell you how to escape a dreadful fate." Lucinda hung her head and continued in despair. "I thought it would be okay, that from my hints, you'd be able to figure out yourself what was going on, and then Sookie would be safe." Lucinda took a deep breath. "But the fairy trick was that when Sookie joined the circle, she fell under the coaches' enchantment. Now she won't listen to me, and she won't listen to you."

As if to prove Lucinda's point, Sookie stuck her tongue out at me.

"To her this is a big adventure, and if you try to drag her away, she'll fight and scream." Lucinda said. "Now she won't try to escape, and I can't leave the circle again." Lucinda stopped swaying, dropped my arm, and began to twirl on the spot.

"Why not?" I whispered. "You managed to escape before!"

"When the veil between both our worlds grew thinner, and the power of Fairy began weakening, I could see into both worlds. I felt a tug when I noticed your little sister sitting on the bleachers. At first I thought she was my sister, Alice, but she wasn't. The bond wasn't strong enough between us, and the power of the circle pulled me back in. And with Sookie here, there's no one tugging me from the outside at all."

Lucinda began to skitter away when she could no longer resist the dance. She managed to twist in my direction and say, "You have to weaken their power over us all. We need a stronger bond to the human world. You have to break the link to Fairy."

I cried out, "How do I do that?"

Lucinda began to tell me, but before she finished a single word, her mouth disappeared! She'd been *forced* to keep her part of the fairy bargain. Terror raced through me as I stared at her.

"Please Sookie, come with me," I shouted.

The stork boy and Grimoire girl slid to a stop, staring at me. They whispered to each other. Sookie simply laughed and joined hands with the two white-haired girls as she spun around and around.

A wave of hopelessness washed over me. How could I fight off these fairies *and* drag my sister and the other girls back to our world? The thing was I couldn't – not alone.

Several fairies moved menacingly toward me, pointing me out and not appreciating that I was trying to break up their diabolical dance. Sweat beaded on my face under my mask, and when I backed away, I stumbled. My mask slid just enough to show a bit of my face. The fairies surged toward me. I turned and ran into the passage.

Reckless now, I leaped up the stairs much faster than I ever had back at Darkmont High, and I yanked up my mask until I could see better. My lungs stung as I breathed in fast and furious gasps while footsteps pounded too closely behind me. Faster, I forced myself up and out into the library. When I grabbed my flashlight out of the door jam, the bookshelf slammed with a huge thud. This time as I passed the grimoire book, I snagged two feather bookmarks and stuffed them into my pocket. If I'd had extra feathers, maybe I could have coaxed Sookie back. Maybe –

The library bookshelf suddenly crashed open behind me.

As I raced out into the corridor, an alarm reverberated through the school. *Clang, clang* it went as the Grimoire students rushed out from the classes. I hurried past, sure that they only could see the back of my head.

Footsteps thundered behind me. "Ms. Peters," shouted my soccer coach. "Come out of your office and grab that student!"

To my utter horror, as I approached the oak door of Grimoire, I could see my mom reflected in the door's glass window. Like someone under a voodoo spell, she marched toward me – my own mother!

I bit my lip until I tasted blood and burst out of the door, hoping she hadn't recognized me.

Afterward, I raced down the hill in the dark, not stopping to catch my breath, not stopping to look where I was going. I tumbled once head over heels, and without missing a beat, was back up and running even harder. All the while I was furious with myself.

It was like taking a shot on goal when I was halfway down the soccer field, with no forwards to pass the ball to and the defense pressing down on me. Do I let the opportunity of making a goal slip by because I'm afraid I'll fail? No, I take a shot. But I hadn't.

Sookie was right there in Fairy, and I didn't grab her, even if it meant throwing her over my shoulder, kicking and screaming, so we could escape. It didn't matter that the odds would have been stacked against me. I had let the opportunity to save my sister slip away.

I passed my house for the second time that night and ran up Fairlane Street. When I burst through the door and into Miss Greystone's front room, she and Jasper were hunched over the computer, staring at the screen. Miss Greystone and Jasper quickly jumped up and rushed toward me.

"Cat, what's …?"

I collapsed on my knees, panting, trying to suck in oxygen.

"We have to go back to the school," I rasped. "We have to free Sookie and the other girls."

CHAPTER 18

An Impossible Challenge

MISS GREYSTONE INSISTED I sit down on her couch and catch my breath before I said anything. The chicken salad sandwich she brought me sat untouched on the plate. I wasn't hungry, but I drank two glasses of water. Besides being freezing cold, the air seemed very dry in Fairy.

Lifting my glass for more water, I told Miss Greystone, "Because you looked a lot like my sister when you were small, Lucinda was able to break free of the fairy circle to talk to Sookie. She thought it was you."

Ms. Greystone and Jasper exchanged confused looks. I took another gulp of water and explained everything that had happened to me.

"That's it!" exclaimed Miss Greystone after I finished my story. She thumped her hand on her fairy tale book. "This book says that the only way to rescue someone from a fairy circle is to create a human chain. Lucinda felt the pull of a little girl she thought was me. She felt the pull of the human heart."

And Sookie's disappearance pulled at my heart every second.

"But Lucinda still couldn't escape," I said quietly, remembering my last horrible moments in Fairy. I didn't mention what the fairies had done to her mouth.

No one spoke for a minute. Finally Jasper said, "Because the pull wasn't strong enough. Maybe if Sookie had been Alice, Lucinda's real sister, Lucinda could have broken free."

I didn't blame them for trying, but they didn't quite understand. They hadn't seen what I had seen, the hideous enchantment that was driving those girls. But then I thought about it.

"Halloween is the key," I decided. "Feeling the pull of the human heart tugs at the enchanted girls. But I also think Lucinda managed to escape in and out of the two worlds because the veil is weaker at this time of year, because it's almost Samhain." I remembered seeing the soccer bleachers superimposed over the fairy field when I was inside the hill. "The barrier between our worlds is becoming thin. Lucinda also mentioned this."

"And while Fairy waits for its new tithe, the fairies grow weaker," said Jasper. "It's as if the batteries are wearing out and its power could shut down." He started pacing again. "Hey, maybe we could break the bridge between the fairy world and here if we convince your soccer team not to play," Jasper said. "No more slaves, right? The link between the netherworld and here would close, and Fairy would have to shut down without any new energy."

For a second, I could almost hear the parts of the puzzle snap into place. Except ... Jasper had missed the most important piece. "But if the link between our worlds closed," I almost shouted, "then how do we get Sookie back?"

"Oh. Right." Jasper looked a bit ashamed.

"Besides," I said, "how would I convince the other girls on my soccer team not to show up? There's nothing that would stop them."

But maybe there was something that could be done. I reached into my pocket and pulled out the other silvery feathers I'd taken from the grimoire book. But seeing through the glamour didn't solve the problem of rescuing Sookie, or saving a new team from being captured and enslaved by Fairy.

"Wait a minute," I said. "Sookie told me when I first started the team that *no one* could win. What if that's it? What if we kept playing the game at a tie, and no one won? The link to Fairy would keep getting weaker and weaker as their power runs out. If no one wins, they can't capture anybody."

Jasper nodded. "And if you could keep the game tied long enough for us to figure out how to make a human chain, we might be able to free Sookie, Lucinda, and her team. If the fairies didn't have slaves at all, wouldn't the link collapse?"

I felt a warm flush of hope.

Jasper suddenly sounded discouraged. "The only thing is that I have no idea how to do it."

Miss Greystone said, "And neither do I."

Maybe, just maybe … I got up, walked over to the mantel, and picked up Miss Greystone's old journal. "Is it possible that some of the brothers and sisters of the people on the old soccer team still live in this town?"

"Very possible," said Miss Greystone. She took the journal and flipped through the pages until she found the section in which she had talked constantly about Lucinda's soccer team. "Madelene Rogers was on that team, and her brother Billy still lives in town. And I play bridge with Pearl's sister, Vivian, every Wednesday night. I'm sure there will be others."

"Here, you'll need this for the brothers and sisters." Handing Miss Greystone an extra feather, I began to form a plan to try to break the fairy spell. We had no choice.

* * *

Later that night when I went home, my mom sat in the living room reading a book. When I came in, she peered over the book cover. "Had the coaches called for evening practice? Good. There's not much time left to get ready for the big day."

I tried to erase the image of her trying to grab

me for the fairies.

Quietly I opened the closet door and buried the black mask under a pile of sweaters. Wearily I climbed the stairs and tugged my shoes off before walking down the hall and into my bedroom. I didn't even finish buttoning my nightgown before I tumbled into bed. That night, I tossed and turned, dreaming I was in the fairy circle.

* * *

When I woke the next morning, at first, I thought that it had all just been a nightmare. Then I remembered that what I had seen could very well be my fate. Sookie had said the school had liked our team's energy the best. The Ghosts played poorly and it was a done deal that our team would win. Jasper and I had to make our plan work, or these would be my last few days of freedom.

While Miss Greystone phoned every single person in town who had had a sister on the original Witches team long ago, Jasper and I plastered every square inch of Darkmont with posters advertising the big game – not that it needed any publicity. The whole town was going to be at the soccer match, and some of our parents and teachers were volunteering to set up the field and act as referees. Secretly I wondered if the Grimoire staff members were becoming too weak and faded to supervise the game. That might be an advantage. Also, we wrote on the poster that only people wearing a Halloween mask would be allowed to watch the game. It was time for this town to take ancient precautions. Besides, it would hide what we were really planning. Once we finished with Darkmont, Jasper and I nailed the posters on every telephone pole and taped them on every shop window and door.

Throughout the week, I forced myself to attend soccer practice so that the coaches wouldn't think that I was onto them. It was the hardest thing I'd ever done in my life. When I crawled out of bed each morning, I wondered how I'd possibly slip on my soccer boots that I'd once loved so much and force a frozen smile on my face as I ran laps around that field. During practice, Ms. Sinster's uncanny stare would drill through the back of my head, and I worried that despite my act, she was becoming suspicious. The only way I managed to keep going was by focusing on one moment at a time.

When I walked to school on Friday, Mr. Keating came out of his emporium.

"Cat," he said as he plucked an apple from his barrel and handed it to me. "I should pay you commission."

"Why?" I asked.

"I've had to order more masks from the next

town. My store has never run out of costumes before, and I hear it was your idea to wear masks to the soccer game."

"Yes," I said, a bit worried about admitting it. "That was me."

Mr. Keating scratched his head. "What a good idea," he said, and his voice drifted. "It's a very good ..." He looked puzzled, then he smiled and walked back into the Emporium.

* * *

The morning of the Halloween soccer match, I called Mia and Amarjeet, as well as Emily from the Ghosts over to my house. When they arrived, I sat them down on my front porch and said, "Before I explain anything, I want you to have these."

I held out the other feather I'd taken from the magic grimoire. Then I took a pair of scissors and cut the feather in three pieces. I handed each girl a piece and told them what I'd discovered about Grim Hill. When I finished, I pointed out certain coincidences.

"Remember your sister's broken engagement, Mia?"

Mia nodded. "Yes, she's been really sad."

"Your dad, Emily," I reminded her. "Remember how after you joined the team, his job sent him up north? How long has it been since you've seen him?"

A tear crept down Emily's face, "A long time."

"And Amarjeet," I hesitated. "Okay, perhaps you don't miss Punjabi school on Saturdays, but when the place burnt down, someone could have been hurt."

"Yes," she nodded. "There were people decorating it for the Diwali festival, and they barely escaped."

"Trust me, none of you wants to win."

At first, they all jumped in at once, disagreeing with me and telling me how the sacrifices they had to make in order to be on the team were nothing compared to how important it was to win the game and the scholarship. But slowly, as they held their feathers, they stopped complaining one by one, and listened with disturbed expressions. I briefly explained the grisly facts about dancing in a fairy ring for the rest of our lives in order to provide strength to the fairies.

"You're kidding. I don't believe any of this," said Mia, but she said it more as if she was *hoping* none of it was true.

"There *is* something wrong with this town," said Amarjeet. "C'mon, face it, nobody has acted normally for weeks."

"And *where did* Sookie go?" Emily agreed quietly. "What is it you want us to do, Cat?"

"Listen, we can't score a goal," I said. "We

have to keep the game tied. The longer no one wins, the weaker the fairy link will become."

"We're in, but what if the Ghosts score a goal?" asked Mia, looking at Emily.

"Never mind that," Emily said. "I've seen you guys play. We haven't got a chance."

Finally I had everything organized – I hoped.

CHAPTER 19

The Execution Begins

ON HALLOWEEN NIGHT, a sickly orange moon rose before the sun went down, and a strange mustard fog wrapped itself around the town, floating up Grim Hill, pointing its foggy fingers at Grimoire School.

I let out a breath as if I'd been holding it all day. "Are we ready?"

"Ready," Jasper and Miss Greystone said in unison as they flashed their feathers, which had now taken on the strange orange moon glow.

"Timing will be everything," I reminded Jasper as I bent down and laced my soccer boots for the fifth time.

"Don't worry," he said, trying to smile.

His expression almost convinced me – Jasper had the heart of a tiger. But even if I wasn't as confident as my friend, our plan *had* to work – or soon I'd be dancing my life away along with Sookie.

"I'd better round up the old folks," fussed Miss Greystone. "I've contacted a sister or brother of every girl on Lucinda's team. Some of them are even coming from out of town for the game." Smiling sadly, she said, "Despite our enchantment,

I think we always knew a big piece of our lives had gone missing. I had no trouble convincing anyone to come." Before Miss Greystone left, she turned to face me and Jasper and grabbed our hands, squeezing them gently. "Cat, Jasper – I'm so glad I met you. Even though it's painful, I'm comforted by the memories of my sister." She hurried off after saying she would meet up with us later at the soccer bleachers.

I let out another breath and looked at Jasper.

"Let's go," he said quietly.

As we climbed Grim Hill to the soccer field, I glanced at the posters we had stapled on every telephone pole.

"This will work," Jasper reassured me.

I shrugged my shoulders. "It's got to." An icy blast blew fiercely on the hill, making me shiver and complain about the cold.

"I read this chill is a *gaoth she*," Jasper explained, tugging up his collar. "A fairy wind blasts when a crossing opens up between our world and Fairy. Ancient Celts used to build hundreds of bonfires on Samhain night to battle the wind, so I organized a bonfire of our own."

Sure enough, a huge bonfire roared at the top of the soccer field with flames shooting up about ten feet in the air, crackling and spitting. I saw Mr. Chung, Jasper's dad, feeding the flames with leaves and branches.

As soon as I joined my soccer team on the field, I slipped my feather into the fold of my sock, securing it behind my shin pad. Mia, Amarjeet, and Emily did the same.

First the townspeople trickled into the field. Jasper shooed anyone away who tried to sit on the bottom of the bleachers, but when I checked a short time later, the whole field had filled, including the bleacher that Jasper had saved. Now the crowds poured in, bunching up along the sidelines. And everyone wore a mask!

Ms. Sinster blew her shrill whistle, and as our team formed a line, the Ghosts ran onto the field. I was playing center, Mia, left forward, and Amarjeet played defense. Emily, the Ghosts' center, stood opposite me.

The second whistle blew. Both Emily and I ran for the ball and both of us kicked – our feet only brushing past each other and the ball not budging an inch.

The crowd howled in disappointment.

Standing in the fog wearing their masks, the townspeople looked a lot more sinister than simply the parents, teachers, and shopkeepers I knew. I shuddered because it was as if I'd time-traveled back to an ancient Celtic village for Samhain. The bonfire that Mr. Chung fed nonstop leaped and cast menacing shadows on everyone.

"We can't get a goal," I said, reminding my

friends of our objective. "No matter what, don't cave in to the pressure." A shout echoed from the bleachers where I spotted my mother, or more accurately, I recognized her voice under a scary metallic robot mask.

"Score, Witches, score!" she urged.

Shaking my head, I reiterated to the others, "We have to keep the game tied, zero - zero. The longer no team wins or pulls ahead, the weaker the fairy link will be." We watched a Ghost girl stumble over her shoelaces. *This shouldn't be too tough.*

The four of us surrounded the ball, cutting off the other Witch girls, but not pushing forward. A surprised Ghost girl came up from behind and lightly tapped the ball, as if she couldn't believe it was just sitting there. The ball trickled forward until Amanda, a Witch girl, shot me a disgusted look before giving the ball a hard kick. I raced after my own team's ball to halt it instead of kick it forward, while Amarjeet and Mia followed behind me. Emily blocked her own team. Both teams were confused. At that point, I overheard the coaches.

"She knows," hissed Ms. Sinster.

"But your whole team isn't playing well," argued Ms. Maliss. "The link must be collapsing."

"Perhaps," Ms. Sinster said loudly in an ominous voice that I think she intended for me to hear.

Our own team now realized they couldn't trust us; they chased ahead trying to get the ball first. A little too late, I realized a flaw in my plan – how hard it would be to keep our own team from scoring.

Mia, Amarjeet, and I did our best, but our team was good. We quickly became exhausted kicking our ball out of bounds, or running offside. The crowd screamed in frustration, and our own team started yelling at us. Finally, when it seemed Mia, Amarjeet, and I could no longer keep our own team at bay, I walked right up to Emily and shoved her. Emily dramatically tumbled down in a heap. A whistle blew. Our ref, Mr. Morrows, came up to me.

"Now, Cat," he said. "I'm sure that was an accident."

I couldn't believe it. Even if he was enchanted, he had to see that was a bad call. Then, right in front of him, I walked over and shoved Emily again. She tumbled down and faked a groan this time.

"Oh, all right," Mr. Morrows sighed. "Ghosts get a penalty shot."

I knew that Emily was getting up slowly so that when she finally got around to taking her shot, she'd kick, miss the goal, and it would be halftime. Then Jasper and I could execute the last half of the plan to destroy the Fairy portal, and the game wouldn't matter anymore.

Then the whistle blew for halftime *before* the Ghosts could take their penalty shot – the coaches and ref appeared to be breaking the rules in order to try and thwart the tied game!

I began to mention the rule, but before I could get a word out, Ms. Sinster hollered, "You're benched, Cat!" She stared at me, making me want to shrivel like a punctured balloon until I shrank from her sight.

Instead, I just said, "Fine." After all, it didn't hurt our plan. As we gathered on the sidelines, Jasper came up and grabbed my arm – it was time. He pointed to the school; you could see right through the stone and brick to the orange moon behind it. The fairy link was weakening! It was now or never.

Behind the lines, Jasper – disguised as a zombie – handed me my black mask, and I led a troop of eleven elderly people up toward the school. Because the whole town was in costume, no one noticed us.

Our masked troop and I crept through the long, checkered corridor and up the stairs to the library, until we piled into the dusty, ancient room and stood in front of the empty bookshelves. Suddenly I realized I'd never actually watched the Grimoire girl open the passageway and had no clue what she'd done. I began to sweat.

"I'm not exactly sure how it works," I said, approaching the bookcase and trying in vain to shove the huge oak case away from the wall.

"There's usually a hidden catch in secret passageways," mentioned Jasper. "At least, that's what I've read."

"He's right," said an elderly man in a Frankenstein mask. "I'm a locksmith, so I could help – but I can't see a thing out of these tiny eyeholes."

There was one shelf that was slightly out of line with the other shelves, so I fiddled with it, tugging and lifting until I heard a click, then the grind and whirr of gears. "Stand back," I said as I jumped away from the swinging door.

Gathering everyone at the top of the passage, I urged, "Whatever you see down there, whatever you do, don't let go of each other's hands. Do *not* break the human chain."

The masks of a witch (Miss Greystone) and the other assorted spooks and ghouls bobbed up and down in agreement.

"When you get to the fairy circle, call out your sisters' names," I explained as I jammed a piece of wood that Jasper had brought to wedge the door open. "Lucinda had no trouble seeing through my disguise, and even though you're all older, I'm sure your sisters will sense you."

"Everyone grab hands. Be careful on the first step," said Miss Greystone.

"Watch out, those steps are steep ... and there might be a few spiders and bats."

"Don't worry, Cat," Ms. Greystone said. "We are too determined to let a few creepy crawlies get to us."

"And I'm in better shape than I look," mentioned a portly woman in a pirate mask.

"So are we," murmured the others.

At that moment, I heard the crowd on the soccer field roar in delight. The library lit up in an unearthly green glow, and the walls of the school became more solid.

"No," I said, realizing that they had resumed the game without me. "Someone must have scored a goal!"

Chapter 20

A Deadly Encounter

THE CROWD'S CHEERS echoed around the library. Getting everyone out of the fairy hill wouldn't matter one bit if a new team of slaves was ready to replace the old one.

"I've got to get back to the game," I said.

"Then I'd better lead everyone into the passage," Jasper said as he stared past the steps that spiraled down into inky darkness.

"Let *me* find the way to Lucinda," said Miss Greystone. "You've got the other whole feather, so you can lead us out.

"Either way," I called after them as I hurried toward the soccer field, "please bring back Sookie."

"Count on it," promised Jasper.

Whatever happened to me then didn't matter. Leaving the school, I pulled off my mask, letting the bitter wind blow across my face. I elbowed my way past the crowd.

When I got back on the soccer field, it became apparent that I hadn't counted on one thing – one very important thing: In its own way, Grimoire School had started to fight back.

The crowd of masked townspeople were still cheering. The players had lined up for a penalty shot. Emily's teammates high-fived her and pounded her on the back. Mia and Amarjeet stared in horror. Emily was crying.

"I'm so sorry," Emily wept. "I haven't been able to kick the ball into the net once this season. I didn't even aim for the goal and the ball just shot in. I'm so sorry."

The tie had been broken. The school pulsed with an eerie green light. Time was running out. We had to score a goal for the Witches – fast.

"C'mon!" I called to Amarjeet and Mia.

"You're supposed to be benched!" screamed Ms. Sinster as I ran onto the field.

I didn't listen. Instead, I whispered to another girl that the coach had called her back.

Mia and I dribbled the ball between us. Amarjeet blocked the Ghosts. Emily blocked her own team. I passed to Mia. She launched the ball and it flew into the Ghosts' net.

We tied!

The crowd screamed and the coaches moaned in disgust.

Now all we had to do was keep the tie going.

It was hard to concentrate. I'd always felt the magic of Halloween night, how it curled around my stomach, buzzed up to my ears, and gave me a light-headed feeling of excitement. I guess humans can sense when the veil between our world and the fairy world is thin. But tonight the magic didn't just buzz – it screamed.

The cold brace of the *gaoth she* actually helped clear my head as I tried to focus. The four of us, the best players on both teams, had to watch our own moves and the moves of eighteen other girls. It was like swimming against a tidal wave. I kept the ball from the Ghosts' right forward and passed to Mia. Amarjeet blocked one of the Witches who tried to take the ball away from Mia.

None of us noticed the other Witch coming up from behind. Amanda whipped the ball from Mia and ran toward the Ghosts' net. Amarjeet and I struck out across the field with Mia following close behind. I dodged in front of Amanda, sending her shot wide. The ball bounced off the goal post, hurtled into the air, then hit Mia. Then the ball ricocheted off Mia's knee and went straight into the Ghosts' goal.

The tie was broken. Witches 2 – Ghosts 1.

The crowd chanted, "Witch-es, Witch-es, Witch-es!"

The coaches cackled in delight. I suddenly began to feel dizzy and my feet throbbed and my legs wanted to kick and dance. I could see right through the bleachers and masked crowds! Behind them, much stranger looking creatures waited for us.

Mia stumbled on the field and had a hard time getting back on her feet.

"I – I see two soccer fields at once," Amarjeet called out in alarm. "Where are the goal posts?"

The door between our two worlds had begun to open.

There was only one thing to do.

Before anyone else could make a move, I grabbed the soccer ball and yelled for everyone to line up.

Mr. Morrows appeared confused, but blew his whistle to start the next play. Emily and I faced off. I got the ball and started dribbling it down the field to my own net.

The crowd and the coaches screamed "No!" and motioned for me to run the other way. The coaches' howls drove ice through my heart. I kept running with the ball and drove it into the Witches' net, scoring on my own goal, scoring a point for the Ghosts. Now we were tied again, 2 – 2.

The queer green light that had been spilling out of the school pulled back. I heard a gigantic pop and the cold, dry fairy wind rushed back up Grim Hill, lifting my hair up off my shoulders, spinning fallen leaves and dirt. I blinked grit from my eyes.

The bonfire that had been burning brightly now began to smoke. The smoke formed the most hideous face I had ever seen – it was like a crazed jack-o'-lantern that had begun to rot. It drifted up from the flames and floated toward me, followed by the two coaches, their claw-like hands ready to grab me.

As the coaches lunged toward me, that horrible pumpkin face grew smoky tendrils of snake-like vines. One tendril brushed against my head. My heart froze and my head ached. The smoke choked me and I couldn't see. From far away, I heard Jasper shout, "Now!"

Miss Greystone and ten masked elderly men and women were rushing out of the school. The old people called out the names of their lost sisters.

"Lucinda, Mary, Mabel, Pearl ... hurry!" they shouted. More people were coming out of the school than had gone in.

The coaches screamed for the other team to stop, but it was already too late. The human chain had worked. Now, because no slaves were left in the fairy hill, the coaches began to fade.

The green light in the school shattered, rays spiked up to the sky in every direction. Then the light pulled back into a fiery ball that spun around, getting smaller and smaller, until it disappeared.

Bricks pounded down onto the ground. Dust rose from the heap, and old men and women, followed by a team of girls, made their way from the ruins of Grimoire to the soccer field.

Strangely, as the girls in the old-fashioned

uniforms approached the bleachers, they grew taller. Then as fast as switching on a light, their hair turned gray and they began to hunch over. Their faces wrinkled like apples left in the sun. By the time the girls reached the bleachers, they'd become a team of elderly women. That is, all but one grew old. A little blond girl trailed behind them. *Sookie!*

The bonfire sputtered out, and there was no longer any sign of the coaches or the crazed jack-o'-lantern. I ran to my little sister, then I grabbed her and hugged her until she squirmed.

"I'm fine," Sookie complained. "I'm thirsty though, and tired – I feel like I haven't slept for days."

An elderly woman who looked very similar to Miss Greystone came and put her arm around Sookie. "But you *have* been awake for days. Remember what I told you – fairy time is different from human time."

Sookie nodded as if she didn't care much, or as if she hadn't even noticed.

Lucinda had aged about seventy years all at once. "You certainly enraged the fairy lord," she said to me. "He left the fairy hill to try and stop you."

I shuddered, remembering the horrible smoke face that had loomed toward me. "That was a pretty close call."

"Closer than you think," said Sookie. She

reached up, grabbed a thick strand of my hair and held it in front of my face. "Look."

My chestnut hair had gone completely ... "Green? My hair's turned green?" I yelled.

"Not all of it." Jasper ran up to reassure me. "Just a few large streaks running along the sides of your head."

"That's where the fairy lord touched you," said Lucinda. "You've been marked by the fairies."

"Green," I muttered.

"It's okay," offered Sookie. "Maybe you can get into the *Guinness Book of World Records* as the only person with naturally green hair."

I couldn't believe this.

The townspeople mingled about in the fog as if they were half in a dream. Nobody even questioned the destruction of Grimoire School, or the soccer game's abrupt end.

"What's happening to them?" I asked, watching girls from both my Witches team and the Ghosts stumble across the field.

Lucinda Greystone shook her head. "Tonight people will go home, sleep deeply, and think the soccer match and the school on the hill were simply dreams. All they'll remember is that a heavy fog rolled in on Halloween night and everybody had to stay home and miss all the fun."

Amarjeet, Mia, and Emily came off the field. The other soccer players caught up with the townsfolk and began making their way down the hill, as did the elderly people who were walking arm in arm.

"We did it," said Mia.

"These feather pieces worked like a charm," said Amarjeet as she dangled hers in front of us. Then she looked at Emily. "Or at least they worked most of the time."

Emily smiled ruefully, walked over, and gave Sookie a hug. "Good to see you again," she said.

Sookie smiled.

"Actually, the feathers worked just fine," said Lucinda Greystone. "The magic of the school was working against the Ghost team," she explained. "Emily's feather allowed her to play well again."

I hadn't thought of that.

"As a matter of fact," said Lucinda, "because these feathers are fairy magic, like all things from Fairy, they are not dependable. They can also be dangerous." She held out her hand and waited as we all turned in our feathers.

I gave up my feather last, but I was happy to leave everything related to Fairy behind – I'd seen enough to realize a charmed life wasn't for me ... except ... if the grimoire's spell had turned me into a soccer star and made me popular, and the fairy feathers had helped me save the town, what was life going to be like now?

CHAPTER 21

Grim Music

THE NEXT MORNING when I woke up and went downstairs for breakfast, Mom was reading the Help Wanted section in the newspaper.

"Interesting hairstyle," she said as she peered over her paper at me.

I shrugged. Even though I'd washed my hair three times that morning, it was still streaked green.

Mom sighed, "My vacation pay is almost spent, so I'd better find a job soon."

Just what did she think she'd been doing the last eight weeks? But I didn't mention anything. Lucinda had said it would all seem like a dream. Sookie came down in her pajamas and poured herself a bowl of cereal.

"Monopoly this Friday?" she yawned. Her eyes had dark circles and she seemed really tired. Otherwise, it was the same old annoying Sookie. I was so happy.

"Yes, we're definitely playing Monopoly," I said. I roughed up her hair as she beamed at me.

But instead of eating her cereal, Sookie stared at the box for a while, getting a dreamy expression on her face. Then she began humming a haunting song that made the hair on my arms and neck prickle.

"Where'd you hear that?" I asked.

"Nowhere," Sookie said, and then she smiled mysteriously.

For a few seconds I stared intently at her, until she laughed and looked more like herself again. I shrugged off the unsettling moment, grabbed my backpack, and was about to leave for school.

"Don't forget you have dishes to do," Mom reminded me.

My hand slipped on the door handle. For weeks I'd been chore free. If only I'd appreciated it more. Marching to the sink, I quickly swished the soap and water, giving the dishes only a soak. "I'll finish up later," I promised.

"Mmm-hmm," Mom muttered behind her newspaper. "The recycling needs sorting as well." Then she gazed out the kitchen window into our backyard. "And later, we'd all better grab a rake and clean up those leaves."

Before Mom remembered any other unfinished chores, I rushed out the door.

All the way to school I was thinking that life without soccer enchantment might take getting used to again. Making a quick stop at the Emporium, I plucked an apple out of the barrel for my lunch.

"That'll be fifty cents." Mr. Keating held out

his hand as I fished through my bag.

At school, as soon as I spun my combination on my locker, I noticed other things had changed. For example, my stupid lock stuck again. It hadn't done that since my first week at Darkmont. Another much more unsettling event happened next. Zach and Mike walked down the hall and right past me, as if I was invisible.

"Hi, Zach," I called after him. If I remembered correctly, he'd invited me to a dance. Zach kept on walking. He didn't even look over his shoulder. Okay, I had to admit that while I was grateful that everyone was acting more normally, I was getting the sense that there was a downside to reality. I couldn't understand how Zach could forget that he was interested in me before. Then I thought about it – it wasn't as if we'd really spent any time together. Sorting out the genuine from the enchanted was confusing.

At least when I went to science class, there was still a seat available for me at Amarjeet's table. However, I wasn't in my seat fifteen seconds before Ms. Dreeble called me to her desk.

"Um ... Cat," she said. "I'm totaling my marks for the midterm report cards, and I've just noticed you have a zero. You'll need to complete eight assignments and have them on my desk tomorrow morning if you want a passing grade."

The magic had *definitely* worn off.

Later, in history class, Mr. Morrows stood over me.

"Cat," he said, "you do realize Halloween is over?"

No kidding, I thought, but I said, "Yes sir, I do."

"Then why have you come to class with your hair striped green?"

The class laughed.

"It's not dyed," I explained. "It's naturally green."

That went over well. I was now standing in the office waiting to see Vice Principal Sevren. When she called me in, I was all prepared to maintain that my hair wasn't dyed, but then I decided I'd just apologize – it would be easier in the long run. It turned out that the subject didn't come up.

"I've checked your records, Caitlin," said Ms. Sevren. "There's a matter of outstanding detentions and a skipped class we have to deal with."

As I wandered back to my locker thinking I was having the worst luck all over again, it finally hit me. *So what* – chores, cute boys ignoring me, homework, detentions. None of that meant anything compared to losing my sister and dancing in a fairy circle for the rest of my life. I finally understood what Mom said about trying to have perspective. I was safe and so was Sookie, and we managed to save other girls as well.

Feeling considerably better, I hurried to the cafeteria for lunch.

At the lunch table, Mia, Amarjeet, and Emily were waiting. I sat down with them, took out the shiny red apple that I'd had to pay for because Mr. Keating wasn't offering any more freebies, and bit into it with a satisfying crunch. Then I asked them, "What's up?"

"You seem cheerful," said Emily. "I thought your day wasn't going so well."

"That depends on how you look at it," I said smiling.

She brightened. "I suppose you have a point. On the one hand, I've got more homework and more detentions than I ever had in my life. On the other hand," she smiled this time and said with barely contained excitement, "my dad's coming into town. We're spending the whole weekend together."

"Perspective," I said.

Mia nodded, understanding, and said, "The wedding's back on for my sister."

"But is anyone having nightmares?" asked Amarjeet. "I'm dreaming about dancing in some kind of circle," she admitted.

By the looks on Emily's and Mia's faces, she wasn't the only one, but I tried to console her. "Lucinda said that because we held the feathers, on one level we will always know we had a close call. But the details will fade soon."

Amarjeet relaxed a bit and said, "They've temporarily relocated the Punjabi school. Who would have thought going back to classes on Saturday would be such a relief?"

Life was getting back to normal and I was happy. Maybe Mom would let me dye my hair completely brown, and if I never heard the word "fairy" again, that would be fine. Maybe we could convince Darkmont to start a soccer team.

Yes, everyone was getting back to life as usual – or almost.

That night as I stayed up late trying to catch up on my homework, a dark, cold melody drifted down the hall and into my bedroom. Restlessness came over me, and I couldn't concentrate. I followed the melody and opened the door to Sookie's room.

She sat beside her window and stared up at Grim Hill, humming a ghostly tune, which was both melancholic and strange. The unsettling part was that I could hardly believe that the haunting music had come from my little sister, and I wondered what she found so interesting outside that window.

"Where'd you hear that song?" I asked.

"I just made it up," said Sookie coyly.

* * *

It wasn't until much later that night, after tons of homework and when I was falling asleep, that I remembered the music. It was similar to the tune the fairies had danced to around their bonfire down inside the hill. I got out of bed and looked out my own window up at Grim Hill. It was mostly dark now, nothing but forest. Except every once in a while, a strange green light flickered on top of the hill. All night I tossed and turned.

The next day at school, I consulted my best friend, Jasper, telling him about Sookie's humming and how at times, she sort of tuned out.

"I've been sort of forgetting about Grim Hill," said Jasper. "Not about what happened, but it feels less real."

"If you listened to Sookie's song, you'd recall more," I said. "You can't miss the weirdness of the melody – that it couldn't possibly be something from our side. Why is Sookie hanging onto that tune? I don't have a good feeling about it."

"Well, there is one expert we could ask," said Jasper. "Maybe Sookie, you, and I should pay a visit to Lucinda Greystone."

* * *

The next day after school, Jasper, Sookie, and I climbed up the porch of Miss Greystone's house on Fairlane Street and rapped on the lion door knocker. Alice Greystone opened the door.

After giving us a warm greeting and ushering us into her front room, she said, "I've just made a pitcher of lemonade."

Lucinda was sitting at the computer desk and swung around on her chair. "Hello," she said smiling. "I've had so much catching up to do."

I mentioned to Lucinda something that had been bothering me. "I'm really sorry you had to grow up a whole lifetime in just a few minutes."

Lucinda gave that some thought. "Even though I saw only seven sunsets when I was in Fairy, I've felt old on the inside for a long time. In a sense, each day there did feel like a decade – and if anything, it seems more like I've lived for a hundred years."

"Really," said Alice, sounding a bit puzzled. "I still feel like my nine-year-old self on the inside."

Lucinda and Miss Greystone told us that what really mattered was the time that they were spending with each other now.

As we all sipped the lemonade, I mentioned that Sookie was humming her strange song and I talked about the light I'd seen on the hill.

Sookie stuck her tongue out at me.

Lucinda put her glass down on a doily and said, "Remember, Sookie, this is your world. This is where you belong."

"I know," said Sookie stubbornly.

"Even though it seemed as if you were in Fairy for only a few minutes," said Lucinda, "it was really almost a week." Then Lucinda turned to me, touched a strand of my green hair, and patted Jasper's hand. "Remember, all of you have been touched by Fairy."

Lucinda stood up, went over to a desk and opened the drawer. She brought out a blue silk handkerchief, unfolded it, and handed us each a silver-white feather.

"I thought you said these could be dangerous," I said, holding my feather as it shimmered mauve and pink.

"There is a potential danger with these feathers," agreed Lucinda. She gave Jasper, Sookie, and me a measured look, sizing us up, I think.

"But there is also danger living near a fairy hill," said Lucinda. "Keep the feathers as tokens of insurance, in case there is ever any more trouble brewing on Grim Hill. And Sookie, keep your feather close to you for a few days." Lucinda unfastened a thin silver chain from her neck and with the tiny clip, hooked the feather onto the chain. "This will help you keep your focus here and will stop you from drifting away and thinking about the hill," she said, lifting back Sookie's hair and slipping the chain around her neck.

"Ah," said Alice Greystone, looking at each of us. "Behold the keepers of the feathers."

Sookie got a mysterious grin on her face again but just nodded. Jasper and I looked at each other. Holding the feather did give me a sense of relief. Everything would be back to normal now.

Right?

THE END

More Fabulous Fantasy from Lobster Press:

The Curious Misadventures of Feltus Ovalton
by Jo Treggiari / ISBN: 978-1-897073-43-8

Ever since he and his parents moved to the city, Feltus Ovalton LeRoi has been hiding out in his room, wishing for something – anything – to happen. With a loud "Wex Lethoo Radok!" his gibberish-speaking, odd-smelling, toad-keeping, Great-Aunt Eunida appears ... and everything changes. Feltus finds himself shoved into the unlikely role of hero, and suddenly, bullies at school and parents that ignore him are the least of his problems!

> "How can someone who can't even go to the boy's bathroom without getting pummeled save an entire world? ... this wildly original book is saturated with dark humor ..."
> – *Chronogram*

> "**Jo Treggiari** has the most imaginatively powerful voice in young people's fiction since the likes of Roald Dahl, Madeleine L'Engle and L. Frank Baum ..."
> – Abigail Thomas, author of **A Three Dog Life**

> " ... exciting, magical, suspenseful, wonderful ... Sophisticated and imaginative, it's the ideal book for smart kids ..."
> – Alison Gaylin, author of **You Kill Me**

The Uncle Duncle Chronicles:
Escape from Treasure Island
by Darren Krill / ISBN: 978-1-897073-31-5

Sage Smiley is going on vacation with his favorite uncle, world-famous explorer Dunkirk Smiley (a.k.a. "Uncle Duncle"), using the powers of a magical talisman to go wherever he wants. But the aerial adventure goes awry when Sage's imagination brings them to Robert Louis Stevenson's **Treasure Island**. Together they must free a group of prisoners from the clutches of Long John Silver, lay claim to the glittering chests of pirate treasure, and fight for their very lives. Does Sage have enough courage and craftiness to survive in this land of legends?

"Non-stop fun and action describes this adventure-filled yarn ..."
– *CM: Canadian Review of Materials*

"[Krill] handles the blend of existing fiction and his own creation beautifully."
– *Children's Literature*

"It's a rollicking adventure ... very exciting, and custom-made to spark the imagination ..."
– *Edmonton Sun*

www.lobsterpress.com

Stolen Voices
by Ellen Dee Davidson / ISBN: 978-1-897073-16-2

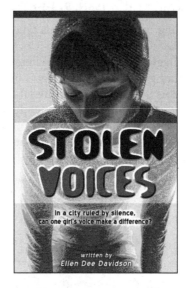

Life in Noveskina is designed to be harmonious and conflict fr
But Miri, daughter of two of the city's Important Officials, fa
a shameful dilemma. She has matured with no clear Talent a
thus faces life among the lower classes. As Miri is confron
with the dark secrets of Noveskina, the quiet peace of her on
perfect world reveals itself as something infinitely more sinis

"... definitely a page-turner that will keep readers captivate
from the start."
– *School Library Journal*

"Set in an intriguing fantasy world, Davidson tells a
compelling story that will strike a chord with many readers
– Pamela F. Service, author of **The Reluctant God**

**Nominated, American Library Association
Amelia Bloomer Project (2006)**

**Selected, International Youth Library's White Ravens
Catalogue, An Annual Selection of International
Children's and Youth Literature**

www.lobsterpress.com